Esther

Henry Adams

Published in 1884 by Henry Holt and Company

Contents

ESTHER

by

Henry Adams

Chapter I

THE new church of St. John's, on Fifth Avenue, was thronged the morning of the last Sunday of October, in the year 1880. Sitting in the gallery, beneath the unfinished frescoes, and looking down the nave, one caught an effect of autumn gardens, a suggestion of chrysanthemums and geraniums, or of October woods, dashed with scarlet oaks and yellow maples. As a display of austerity the show was a failure, but if cheerful content and innocent adornment please the Author of the lilies and roses, there was reason to hope that this first service at St. John's found favor in his sight, even though it showed no victory over the world or the flesh in this part of the United States. The sun came in through the figure of St. John in his crimson and green garments of glass, and scattered more color where colors already rivaled the flowers of a prize show; while huge prophets and evangelists in flowing robes looked down from the red walls on a display of human vanities that would have called out a vehement Lamentation of Jeremiah or Song of Solomon, had these poets been present in flesh as they were in figure.

Solomon was a brilliant but not an accurate observer; he looked at the world from the narrow stand-point of his own temple. Here in New York he could not have truthfully said that all was vanity, for even a more ill-natured satirist than he must have confessed that there was in this new temple to-day a perceptible interest in religion. One might almost have said that religion seemed to be a matter of concern. The audience wore a look of interest, and, even after their first gaze of admiration and whispered criticism at the splendors of their new church, when at length the clergyman entered to begin the service, a ripple of excitement swept across the field of bonnets until there was almost a murmur as of rustling cornfields within the many colored walls of St. John's.

In a remote pew, hidden under a gallery of the transept, two persons looked on with especial interest. The number of strangers who crowded in after them forced them to sit closely together, and their low whispers of comment were unheard by their neighbors. Before the service began they talked in a secular tone.

"Wharton's window is too high-toned," said the man.

"You all said it would be like Aladdin's," murmured the woman.

"Yes, but he throws away his jewels," rejoined the man. "See the big prophet over the arch; he looks as though he wanted to come down--and I think he ought."

"Did Michael Angelo ever take lessons of Mr. Wharton?" asked the woman seriously, looking up at the figures high above the pulpit.

"He was only a prophet," answered her companion, and, looking in another direction, next asked:

"Who is the angel of Paradise, in the dove-colored wings, sliding up the main aisle?"

"That! O, you know her! It is Miss Leonard. She is lovely, but she is only an angel of Paris."

"I never saw her before in my life," he replied; "but I know her bonnet was put on in the Lord's honor for the first time this morning."

"Women should take their bonnets off at the church door, as Mussulmen do their shoes," she answered.

"Don't turn Mahommedan, Esther. To be a Puritan is bad enough. The bonnets match the decorations."

"Pity the transepts are not finished!" she continued, gazing up at the bare scaffolding opposite.

"You are lucky to have any thing finished," he rejoined. "Since Hazard got here every thing is turned upside down; all the plans are changed. He and Wharton have taken the bit in their teeth, and the church committee have got to pay for whatever damage is done."

"Has Mr. Hazard voice enough to fill the church?" she asked.

"Watch him, and see how well he'll do it. Here he comes, and he will hit the right pitch on his first word."

The organ stopped, the clergyman appeared, and the talkers were silent until the litany ended and the organ began again. Under the prolonged rustle of settling for the sermon, more whispers passed.

"He is all eyes," murmured Esther; and it was true that at this distance the preacher seemed to be made up of two eyes and a voice, so slight and delicate was his frame. Very tall, slender and dark, his thin, long face gave so spiritual an expression to his figure that the great eyes seemed to penetrate like his clear voice to every soul within their range.

"Good art!" muttered her companion.

"We are too much behind the scenes," replied she.

"It is a stage, like any other," he rejoined; "there should be an entre-acte and drop-scene. Wharton could design one with a last judgment."

"He would put us into it, George, and we should be among the wicked."

"I am a martyr," answered George shortly.

The clergyman now mounted his pulpit and after a moment's pause said in his quietest manner and clearest voice:

"He that hath ears to hear, let him hear."

An almost imperceptible shiver passed through Esther's figure.

"Wait! he will slip in the humility later," muttered George.

On the contrary, the young preacher seemed bent on letting no trace of humility slip into his first sermon. Nothing could be simpler than his manner, which, if it had a fault, sinned rather on the side of plainness and monotony than of rhetoric, but he spoke with the air of one who had a message to deliver which he was more anxious to give as he received than to add any thing of his own; he meant to repeat it all without an attempt to soften it. He took possession of his flock with a general advertisement that he owned every sheep in it, white or black, and to show that there could be no doubt on the matter, he added a general claim to right of property in all mankind and the universe. He did this in the name and on behalf of the church universal, but there was self-assertion in the quiet air with which he pointed out the nature of his title, and then, after sweeping all human thought and will into his strong-box, shut down the lid with a sharp click, and bade his audience kneel.

The sermon dealt with the relations of religion to society. It began by claiming that all being and all thought rose by slow gradations to God,--ended in Him, for Him--existed only through Him and because of being His.

The form of act or thought mattered nothing. The hymns of David, the plays of

Shakespeare, the metaphysics of Descartes, the crimes of Borgia, the virtues of An-
tonine, the atheism of yesterday and the materialism of to-day, were all emanations
of divine thought, doing their appointed work. It was the duty of the church to
deal with them all, not as though they existed through a power hostile to the deity,
but as instruments of the deity to work out his unrevealed ends. The preacher then
went on to criticise the attitude of religion towards science. "If there is still a feeling
of hostility between them," he said, "it is no longer the fault of religion. There have
been times when the church seemed afraid, but she is so no longer. Analyze, dissect,
use your microscope or your spectrum till the last atom of matter is reached; reflect
and refine till the last element of thought is made clear; the church now knows
with the certainty of science what she once knew only by the certainty of faith, that
you will find enthroned behind all thought and matter only one central idea,--that
idea which the church has never ceased to embody,--I AM! Science like religion
kneels before this mystery; it can carry itself back only to this simple consciousness
of existence. I AM is the starting point and goal of metaphysics and logic, but the
church alone has pointed out from the beginning that this starting-point is not human but divine. The philosopher says--I am, and the church scouts his philosophy.
She answers:--No! you are NOT, you have no existence of your own. You were and
are and ever will be only a part of the supreme I AM, of which the church is the
emblem."

In this symbolic expression of his right of property in their souls and bodies,
perhaps the preacher rose a little above the heads of his audience. Most of his flock
were busied with a kind of speculation so foreign to that of metaphysics that they
would have been puzzled to explain what was meant by Descartes' famous COGITO
ERGO SUM, on which the preacher laid so much stress. They would have preferred
to put the fact of their existence on almost any other experience in life, as that "I
have five millions," or, "I am the best-dressed woman in the church,--therefore I
am somebody." The fact of self-consciousness would not have struck them as war-
ranting a claim even to a good social position, much less to a share in omnipotence;
they knew the trait only as a sign of bad manners. Yet there were at least two persons among the glorified chrysanthemums of St. John's Garden this day, who as the
sermon closed and the organ burst out again, glanced at each other with a smile as
though they had enjoyed their lecture.

"Good!" said the man. "He takes hold."

"I hope he believes it all," said his companion.

"Yes, he has put his life into the idea," replied the man. "Even at college he would have sent us all off to the stake with a sweet smile, for the love of Christ and the glory of the English Episcopal Church."

The crowd soon began to pour slowly out of the building and the two observers were swept along with the rest until at length they found themselves outside, and strolled down the avenue. A voice from behind stopped them.

"Esther!" it called.

Esther turned and greeted the caller as aunt. She was a woman of about fifty, still rather handsome, but with features to which time had given an expression of character and will that harmonized only with a manner a little abrupt and decided. She had the air of a woman who knew her own mind and commonly had her own way.

"Well, Esther, I am glad to see you taking George to church. Has he behaved himself?"

"You are wrong again, Aunt Sarah," said George; "it is I who have been taking Esther to church. I thought it was worth seeing."

"Church is always worth seeing, George, and I hope your friend Mr. Hazard's sermon has done you good."

"It did me good to see Wharton there," answered George; "he looked as though it were a first representation, and he were in a stage box. Hazard and he ought to have appeared before the curtain, hand in hand, and made little speeches. I felt like calling them out."

"What did you think of it, Esther?" asked her aunt.

"I thought it very entertaining, Aunt Sarah. I felt like a butterfly in a tulip bed. Mr. Hazard's eyes are wonderful."

"I shall never get you two to be reverential," said her aunt sternly. "It was the best sermon I ever heard, and I would like to hear you answer it, George, and make your answer as little scientific as you can."

"Aunt Sarah, I never answered any one in my life, not even you, or Esther, or the man who said that my fossil bird was a crocodile. Why do you want me to answer him?"

"Because I don't believe you can."

"I can't. I am a professor of paleontology at the college, and I answer questions about bones. You must get my colleague who does the metaphysics to answer Hazard's sermon. Hazard and I have had it out fifty times, and discussed the whole subject till night reeled, but we never got within shouting distance of each other. He might as well have stood on the earth, and I on the nearest planet, and bawled across. So we have given it up."

"You mean that you were beaten," rejoined his aunt. "I am glad you feel it, though I always knew it was so. After all, Mr. Hazard has got more saints on his church walls than he will ever see in his audience, though not such pretty ones. I never saw so many lovely faces and dresses together. Esther, how is your father today?"

"Not very well, aunt. He wants to see you. Come home with us and help us to amuse him."

So talking, all three walked along the avenue to 42d Street, and turning down it, at length entered one of the houses about half way between the avenues. Upstairs in a sunny room fitted up as a library and large enough to be handsome, they found the owner, William Dudley, a man of sixty or thereabouts, sitting in an arm-chair before the fire, trying to read a foreign review in which he took no interest. He moved with an appearance of effort, as though he were an invalid, but his voice was strong and his manner cheerful.

"I hoped you would all come. This is an awful moment. Tell me instantly, Sarah; is St. Stephen a success?"

"Immense! St. Stephen and St. Wharton too. The loveliest clergyman, the sweetest church, the highest-toned sermon and the lowest-toned walls," said she. "Even George owns that he has no criticisms to make."

"Aunt Sarah tells the loftiest truth, Uncle William," said the professor; "every Christian emblem about the church is superlatively correct, but paleontologically it is a fraud. Wharton and Hazard did the emblems, and I supplied them with antediluvian beasts which were all right when I drew them, but Wharton has played the devil with them, and I don't believe he knows the difference between a saurian and a crab. I could not recognize one of my own offspring."

"And how did it suit you, Esther?"

"I am charmed," replied his daughter. "Only it certainly does come just a little near being an opera-house. Mr. Hazard looks horribly like Meyerbeer's Prophet. He ordered us about in a fine tenor voice, with his eyes, and told us that we belonged to him, and if we did not behave ourselves he would blow up the church and us in it. I thought every moment we should see his mother come out of the front pews, and have a scene with him. If the organ had played the march, the effect would have been complete, but I felt there was something wanting."

"It was the sexton," said the professor; "he ought to have had a medieval costume. I must tell Wharton to-night to invent one for him. Hazard has asked me to come round to his rooms, because he thinks I am an unprejudiced observer and will tell him the exact truth. Now what am I to say?"

"Tell him," said the aunt, "that he looked like a Christian martyr defying the beasts in the amphitheater, and George, you are one of them. Between you and your Uncle William I wonder how Esther and I keep any religion at all."

"It is not enough to save you, Aunt Sarah," replied the professor. "You might just as well go with us, for if the Church is half right, you haven't a chance."

"Just now I must go with my husband, who is not much better than you," she replied. "He must have his luncheon, church or no church. Good-by."

So she departed, notifying Esther that the next day there was to be at her house a meeting of the executive committee of the children's hospital, which Esther must be careful to attend.

When she was out of the room the professor turned to his uncle and said: "Seriously, Uncle William, I wish you knew Stephen Hazard. He is a pleasant fellow in or out of the pulpit, and would amuse you. If you and Esther will come to tea some afternoon at my rooms, I will get Hazard and Wharton and Aunt Sarah there to meet you."

"Will he preach at me?" asked Mr. Dudley.

"Never in his life," replied the professor warmly. "He is the most rational, unaffected parson in the world. He likes fun as much as you or any other man, and is interested in every thing."

"I will come if Esther will let me," said Mr. Dudley. "What have you to say about it, Esther?"

"I don't think it would hurt you, father. George's building has an elevator."

"I didn't mean that, you watch-dog. I meant to ask whether you wanted to go to George's tea party?"

"I should like it of all things. Mr. Hazard won't hurt me, and I always like to meet Mr. Wharton."

"Then I will ask both of them this evening for some day next week or the week after, and will let you know," said George.

"Is he easily shocked?" asked Mr. Dudley. "Am I to do the old-school Puritan with him, or what?"

"Stephen Hazard," replied the professor, "is as much a man of the world as you or I. He is only thirty-five; we were at college together, took our degrees together, went abroad at the same time, and to the same German university. He had then more money than I, and traveled longer, went to the East, studied a little of every thing, lived some time in Paris, where he discovered Wharton, and at last some few years ago came home to take a church at Cincinnati, where he made himself a power. I thought he made a mistake in leaving there to come to St. John's, and wrote him so. I thought if he came here he would find that he had no regular community to deal with but just an Arab horde, and that it was nonsense to talk of saving the souls of New Yorkers who have no souls to be saved. But he thought it his duty to take the offer. Aunt Sarah hit it right when she called him a Christian martyr in the amphitheater. At college, we used to call him St. Stephen. He had this same idea that the church was every thing, and that every thing belonged to the church. When I told him that he was a common nuisance, and that I had to work for him like a church-warden, he laughed as though it were a joke, and seriously told me it was all right, and he didn't mind my skepticism at all. I know he was laughing at me this morning, when he made me go to church for the first time in ten years to hear that sermon which not twenty people there understood."

"One always has to pay for one's friend's hobbies," said Mr. Dudley. "I am glad he has had a success. If we keep a church we ought to do it in the best style. What will you give me for my pew?"

"I never sat in a worse," growled Strong.

"I'll not change it then," said Mr. Dudley. "I'll make Esther use it to mortify her pride."

"Better make it over to the poor of the parish," said the professor; "you will get no thanks for it even from them."

Mr. Dudley laughed as though it were no affair of his, and in fact he never sat in his pew, and never expected to do so; he had no taste for church-going. A lawyer in moderate practice, with active interest in public affairs, when the civil war broke out he took a commission as captain in a New York regiment, and, after distinguishing himself, was brought home, a colonel, with a bullet through his body and a saber cut across his head. He recovered his health, or as much of it as a man can expect to recover after such treatment, and went back to the law, but coming by inheritance into a property large enough to make him indifferent to his profession, and having an only child whose mother was long since dead, he amused the rest of his life by spoiling this girl. Esther was now twenty-five years old, and for fifteen years had been absolute mistress of her father's house. Her Aunt Sarah, known in New York as Mrs. John Murray of 53d Street, was the only person of whom she was a little--a very little--afraid. Of her Cousin George she was not in the least afraid, although George Strong spoke with authority in the world when he cared to speak at all. He was rich, and his professorship was little more to him than a way of spending money. He had no parents, and no relations besides the Dudleys and the Murrays. Alone in the world, George Strong looked upon himself as having in Esther a younger sister whom he liked, and a sort of older sister, whom he also liked, in his Aunt Sarah.

When, after lunching with the Dudleys, Professor Strong walked down Fifth Avenue to his club, he looked, to the thousand people whom he passed, like what he was, an intelligent man, with a figure made for action, an eye that hated rest, and a manner naturally sympathetic. His forehead was so bald as to give his face a look of strong character, which a dark beard rather helped to increase. He was a popular fellow, known as George by whole gangs of the roughest miners in Nevada, where he had worked for years as a practical geologist, and it would have been hard to find in America, Europe, or Asia, a city in which some one would not have smiled at the mention of his name, and asked where George was going to turn up next.

He kept his word that evening with his friend Hazard. At nine o'clock he was at the house, next door to St. John's church, where the new clergyman was trying to feel himself at home. In a large library, with book-cases to the ceiling, and books lying in piles on the floor; with pictures, engravings and etchings leaning against the books and the walls, and every sort of literary encumbrance scattered in the way of heedless feet; in the midst of confusion confounded, Mr. Hazard was stretched on a sofa trying to read, but worn out by fatigue and excitement. Though his chaos had not settled into order, it was easy to read his character from his surroundings. The books were not all divinity. There were classics of every kind, even to a collection of Eastern literature; a mass of poetry in all languages; not a few novels; and what was most conspicuous, an elaborate collection of illustrated works on art, Egyptian, Greek, Roman, Medieval, Mexican, Japanese, Indian, and whatever else had come in his way. Add to this a shelf of music, and then--construct the tall, slender, large-eyed, thin-nosed, dark-haired figure lying exhausted on the sofa.

He rose to greet Strong with a laugh like a boy, and cried: "Well, skeptic, how do the heathen rage?"

"The heathen are all right," replied Strong. "The orthodox are the ragers."

"Never mind the orthodox," said Hazard. "I will look after them. Tell me about the Pagans. I felt like St. Paul preaching at Athens the God whom they ignorantly worshiped."

"I took with me the sternest little Pagan I know, my cousin, Esther Dudley," said Strong; "and the only question she asked was whether you believed it all."

"She hit the mark at the first shot," answered Hazard. "I must make them all ask that question. Tell me about your cousin. Who is she? Her name sounds familiar."

"As familiar as Hawthorne," replied Strong. "One of his tales is called after it. Her father comes from a branch of the old Puritan Dudleys, and took a fancy to the name when he met it in Hawthorne's story. You never heard of them before because you have been always away from New York, and when you were here they happened to be away. You know that half a dozen women run this city, and my aunt, Mrs. Murray, is one of the half-dozen. She is training Esther to take her place when she retires. I want you to know my Uncle Dudley and my cousin. I am going to have a little tea-party for them in my rooms, and you must help me with it."

Mr. Hazard asked only to have it put off until the week after the next because of his engagements, and hardly had they fixed the day when another caller appeared.

He was a man of their own age, so quiet and subdued in manner, and so delicate in feature, that he would have been unnoticed in any ordinary group, and shoved aside into a corner. He seemed to face life with an effort; his light-brown eyes had an uneasy look as though they wanted to rest on something that should be less hard and real than what they saw. He was not handsome; his mouth was a little sensual; his yellowish beard was ragged. He was apt to be silent until his shyness wore off, when he became a rapid, nervous talker, full of theories and schemes, which he changed from one day to another, but which were always quite complete and convincing for the moment. At times he had long fits of moodiness and would not open his mouth for days. At other times he sought society and sat up all night talking, planning, discussing, drinking, smoking, living on bread and cheese or whatever happened to be within reach, and sleeping whenever he happened to feel in the humor for it. Rule or method he had none, and his friends had for years given up the attempt to control him. They took it for granted that he would soon kill himself with his ill-regulated existence. Hazard thought that his lungs would give way, and Strong insisted that his brain was the weak spot, and no one ventured to hope that he would long hold out, but he lived on in defiance of them.

"Good evening, Wharton," said the clergyman. "I have been trying to find out from Strong what the heathen think of me. Tell us now the art view of the case. How are you satisfied?"

"Tell me what you were sketching in church," said Strong. "Was it not the new martyrdom of St. Stephen?"

"No," answered Wharton quietly. "It was my own. I found I could not look up; I knew how bad my own work was, and I could not stand seeing it; so I drew my own martyrdom rather than make a scandal by leaving the church."

"Did you hear my sermon?" asked the clergyman.

"I don't remember," answered Wharton vaguely; "what was it about?"

Strong and Hazard broke into a laugh which roused him to the energy of self-defense.

"I never could listen," he said. "It is a slow and stupid faculty. An artist's business is only to see, and to-day I could see nothing but my own things which are all bad. The whole church is bad. It is not altogether worth a bit of Japanese enamel that I have brought round here this evening to show Strong."

He searched first in one pocket, then in another, until he found what he wanted in the pocket of his overcoat, and a warm discussion at once began between him and Strong, who declared that he had a better piece.

"Mine was given me by a Daimio, in Kiusiu," said Strong. "It is the best old bit you ever saw. Come round to my rooms a week from to-morrow at five o'clock in the afternoon, and I will show you all my new japs. The Dudleys are coming to see them, and my aunt Mrs. Murray, and Hazard has promised to come."

"I saw you had Miss Dudley with you at church this morning," said Wharton, still absorbed in study of his enamel, and quite unconscious of his host's evident restlessness.

"Ah! then you could see Miss Dudley!" cried the clergyman, who could not forgive the abrupt dismissal of his own affairs by the two men, and was eager to bring the talk back to his church.

"I can always see Miss Dudley," said Wharton quietly.

"Why?" asked Hazard.

"She is interesting," replied the painter. "She has a style of her own, and I never can quite make up my mind whether to like it or not."

"It is the first time I ever knew you to hesitate before a style," said Hazard.

"I hesitate before every thing American," replied Wharton, beginning to show a shade of interest in what he was talking of. "I don't know--you don't know--and I never yet met any man who could tell me, whether American types are going to supplant the old ones, or whether they are to come to nothing for want of ideas. Miss Dudley is one of the most marked American types I ever saw."

"What are the signs of the most marked American type you ever saw?" asked Hazard.

"In the first place, she has a bad figure, which she makes answer for a good one. She is too slight, too thin; she looks fragile, willowy, as the cheap novels call it, as though you could break her in halves like a switch. She dresses to suit her figure and sometimes overdoes it. Her features are imperfect. Except her ears, her voice, and her eyes which have a sort of brown depth like a trout brook, she has no very good points."

"Then why do you hesitate?" asked Strong, who was not entirely pleased with this cool estimate of his cousin's person.

"There is the point where the subtlety comes in," replied the painter. "Miss Dudley interests me. I want to know what she can make of life. She gives one the idea of a lightly-sparred yacht in mid-ocean; unexpected; you ask yourself what the devil she is doing there. She sails gayly along, though there is no land in sight and plenty of rough weather coming. She never read a book, I believe, in her life. She tries to paint, but she is only a second rate amateur and will never be any thing more, though she has done one or two things which I give you my word I would like to have done myself. She picks up all she knows without an effort and knows nothing well, yet she seems to understand whatever is said. Her mind is as irregular as her face, and both have the same peculiarity. I notice that the lines of her eyebrows, nose and mouth all end with a slight upward curve like a yacht's sails, which gives a kind of hopefulness and self-confidence to her expression. Mind and face have the same curves."

"Is that your idea of our national type?" asked Strong. "Why don't you put it into one of your saints in the church, and show what you mean by American art?"

"I wish I could," said the artist. "I have passed weeks trying to catch it. The thing is too subtle, and it is not a grand type, like what we are used to in the academies. But besides the riddle, I like Miss Dudley for herself. The way she takes my brutal criticisms of her painting makes my heart bleed. I mean to go down on my knees one of these days, and confess to her that I know nothing about it; only if her style is right, my art is wrong."

"What sort of a world does this new deity of yours belong to?" asked the clergyman.

"Not to yours," replied Wharton quickly. "There is nothing medieval about her. If she belongs to any besides the present, it is to the next world which artists want to see, when paganism will come again and we can give a divinity to every waterfall. I tell you, Hazard, I am sick at heart about our church work; it is a failure. Never till this morning did I feel the whole truth, but the instant I got inside the doors it flashed upon me like St. Paul's great light. The thing does not belong to our time or feelings."

The conversation having thus come round to the subject which Mr. Hazard wanted to discuss, the three men plunged deep into serious talk which lasted till after midnight had struck from the neighboring church.

Chapter II

PUNCTUALLY the next day at three o'clock, Esther Dudley appeared in her aunt's drawing-room where she found half a dozen ladies chatting, or looking at Mr. Murray's pictures in the front parlor. The lady of the house sat in an arm-chair before the fire in an inner room, talking with two other ladies of the board, one of whom, with an aggressive and superior manner, seemed finding fault with every thing except the Middle Ages and Pericles.

"A tailor who builds a palace to live in," said she, "is a vulgar tailor, and an artist who paints the tailor and his palace as though he were painting a doge of Venice, is a vulgar artist."

"But, Mrs. Dyer," replied her hostess coldly, "I don't believe there was any real difference between a doge of Venice and a doge of New York. They all made fortunes more or less by cheating their neighbors, and when they were rich they wanted portraits. Some one told them to send for Mr. Tizian or Mr. Wharton, and he made of them all the gentlemen there ever were."

Mrs. Dyer frowned a protest against this heresy. "Tizian would have respected his art," said she; "these New York men are making money."

"For my part," said Mrs. Murray as gently as she could, "I am grateful to any one who likes beautiful things and is willing to pay for them, and I hope the artists will make them as beautiful as they can for the money. The number is small."

With this she rose, and moving to the table, called her meeting to order. The ladies seated themselves in a business-like way round about, and listened with masculine gravity to a long written report on the work done or needing to be done at the Children's Hospital. Debate rose on the question of putting in a new kitchen range and renewing the plumbing. Mrs. Dyer took the floor, or the table, very much to herself, dealing severely with the treatment of the late kitchen range, and bringing numerous complaints against the matron, the management and the hospital in general. There was an evident look of weariness on the part of the board when she began, but not until after a two hours' session did she show signs of exhaustion and allow a vote to be taken. The necessary work was then rapidly done, and at last Mrs. Murray, referring in a business-like way to her notes, remarked that she had nothing more to suggest except that Mr. Hazard, the new clergyman at St. John's, should be elected as a member of their visiting committee.

"Do we want more figure-heads there?" asked Mrs. Dyer. "Every day and every hour of Mr. Hazard's time ought to be devoted to his church. What we want is workers. We have no one to look after the children's clothes and go down into the kitchen. All our visitors are good for is to amuse the children for half an hour now and then by telling them stories."

Mrs. Murray explained that the election was rather a matter of custom; that the rector of St. John's always had been a member of their committee, and it would look like a personal slight if they left him off; so the vote was passed and the meeting broke up. When the last echo of rapid talk and leave-taking had ceased, Mrs. Murray sat down again before the fire with the air of one who has tried to keep her temper and has not thoroughly satisfied her ambition.

"Mrs. Dyer is very trying," she said to Esther who stayed after the others went; "but there is always one such woman on every board. I should not care except that she gives me a dreadful feeling that I am like her. I hope I'm not, but I know I am."

"You're not, Aunt Sarah!" replied Esther. "She can stick pins faster and deeper than a dozen such as you. What makes me unhappy is that her spitefulness goes so deep. Her dig at me about telling stories to the children seemed to cut me up by the roots. All I do is to tell them stories."

"I hope she will never make herself useful in that way," rejoined Mrs. Murray grimly. "She would frighten the poor little things into convulsions. Don't let her worry you about usefulness. One of these days you will have to be useful whether you like it or not, and now you are doing enough if you are only ornamental. I know you will hold your tongue at the board meetings, and that is real usefulness."

"Very well, aunt! I can do that. And I can go on cutting out dolls' clothes for the children, though Mrs. Dyer will complain that my dolls are not sufficiently dressed.

I wish I did not respect people for despising me."

"If we did not, there would be no Mrs. Dyers," answered her aunt. "She is a terrible woman. I feel always like a sort of dry lamp-wick when she has left me. Never mind! I have something else now to talk about. I want you to make yourself useful in a harder path."

"Not another Charity Board, aunt," said Esther rather piteously.

"Worse!" said Mrs. Murray. "A charity girl! Thirty years ago I had a dear friend who was also a friend of your poor mother's. Her name was Catherine Cortright. She married a man named Brooke, and they went west, and they kept going further and further west until at length they reached Colorado, where she died, leaving one daughter, a child of ten years old. The father married again and had a new family. Very lately he has died, leaving the girl with her step-mother and half-sisters. She is unhappy there; they seem to have brought her up in a strict Presbyterian kind of way, and she does not like it. Mr. Murray is an executor under her father's will, and when she comes of age in a few months, she will have a little independent property. She has asked me to look after her till then, and is coming on at once to make me a visit."

"You are always doing something for somebody," said Esther. "What do you expect her to be, and how long will she stay?"

"I don't expect any thing, my dear, and my heart sinks whenever I think of her. My letters say she is amiable and pretty; but if she is a rattlesnake, I must take her in, and you must help to amuse her."

"I will do all I can," replied Esther. "Don't be low about it. She can't be as bad as Mrs. Dyer even if she is a rattlesnake. If she is pretty, and turns out well, we will make George marry her."

"I wish we might," said her aunt.

Esther went her way and thought no more of the orphan, but Mrs. Murray carried the weight of all New York on her mind. Not the least of her anxieties was the condition of her brother-in-law, Esther's father. He was now a confirmed invalid, grateful for society and amusement, and almost every day he expected his sister-in-law to take him to drive, if the weather was tolerable. The tax was severe, but she bore it with heroism, and his gratitude sustained her. When she came for him the next morning, she found him reading as usual, and waiting for her. "I was just wondering," said he, "whether I could read five minutes longer without a stimulant. Do you know that indiscriminate reading is a fiendish torture. No convict could stand it. I seldom take up a book in these days without thinking how much more amusing it would be to jolt off on a bright day at the head of a funeral procession. Between the two ways of amusing one's-self, I am principled against books."

"You have a very rough way of expressing your tastes," said Mrs. Murray with a shiver, as they got into her carriage. "Do you know, I never could understand the humor of joking about funerals."

"That surprises me," said Mr. Dudley. "A good funeral needs a joke. If mine is not more amusing than my friends', I would rather not go to it. The kind of funeral I am invited to has no sort of charm. Indeed, I don't know that I was ever asked to one that seemed to me to show an elegant hospitality in the host."

"If you can't amuse me better, William, I will drive you home again," said his sister-in-law.

"Not quite yet. I have something more to say on this business of funerals which is just now not a little on my mind."

"Are you joking now, or serious?" asked Mrs. Murray.

"I cannot myself see any humor in what I have to say," replied Mr. Dudley; "but I am told that even professional humorists seldom enjoy jokes at their own expense. The case is this. My doctors, who give me their word of honor that they are not more ignorant than the average of their profession, told me long ago that I might die at any moment. I knew then that I must be quite safe, and thought no more about it. Their first guess was wrong. Instead of going off suddenly and without notice, as a colonel of New York volunteers should, I began last summer to go off by bits, as though I were ashamed to be seen running away. This time the doctors won't say any thing, which alarms me. I have watched myself and them for some weeks until I feel pretty confident that I had better get ready to start. All through life I have been thinking how I could best get out of it, and on the whole I am well enough satisfied with this way, except on Esther's account, and it is about her that I want to consult you."

Mrs. Murray knew her brother-in-law too well to irritate him by condolence or sympathy. She said only: "Why be anxious? Esther can take care of herself. Perhaps she will marry, but if not, she has nothing to fear. The unmarried women nowadays are better off than the married ones."

"Oh!" said Mr. Dudley with his usual air of deep gravity; "it is not she, but her husband who is on my mind. I have hated the fellow all his life. About twice a year I have treacherously stabbed him in the back as he was going out of my own front door. I knew that he would interfere with my comfort if I let him get a footing. After all he was always a poor creature, and did not deserve to live. My conscience does not reproach me. But now, when I am weak, and his ghost rises in an irrepressible manner, and grins at me on my own threshold, I begin to feel a sort of pity, mingled with contempt. I want to show charity to him before I die."

"What on earth do you mean?" asked his sister-in-law with an impatient groan. "For thirty years I have been trying to understand you, and you grow worse every year."

"Now, I am not surprised to hear you say so. Any sympathy for the husband is unusual, no doubt, yet I am not prepared to admit that it is unintelligible. You go too far."

"Take your own way, William. When you are tired, let me know what it is that you think I can do."

"I want you to find the poor fellow, and tell him that I bear him no real ill-will."

"You want me to find a husband for Esther?"

"If you have nothing better to do. I have looked rather carefully through her list of friends, and, taking out the dancing men who don't count, I see nobody who would answer, except perhaps her Cousin George, and to marry him would be cold-blooded. She might as well marry you."

"I have thought a great deal about that match, as you know," replied Mrs. Murray. "It would not answer. I could get over the cousinship, if I must, but Esther will want a husband to herself and George is a vagabond. He could never make her happy."

"George had the ill-luck," said Mr. Dudley, "to inherit a small spark of something almost like genius; and a little weak genius mixed in with a little fortune, goes a long way towards making a jack-o-lantern. Still we won't exaggerate George's genius. After all there is not enough of it to prevent his being the best of the lot."

"He could not hold her a week," said Mrs. Murray; "nor she him."

"I own that on his wedding day he would probably be in Dakota flirting with the bones of a fossil monkey," said Mr. Dudley thoughtfully; "but what better can you suggest?"

"I suggest that you should leave it alone, and let Esther take care of her own husband," replied Mrs. Murray. "Women must take their chance. It is what they are for. Marriage makes no real difference in their lot. All the contented women are fools, and all the discontented ones want to be men. Women are a blunder in the creation, and must take the consequences. If Esther is sensible she will never marry; but no woman is sensible, so she will marry without consulting us."

"You are always eloquent on this subject," said Mr. Dudley. "Why have you never applied for a divorce from poor Murray?"

"Because Mr. Murray happens to be one man in a million," answered she. "Nothing on earth would induce me to begin over again and take such a risk a second time, with life before me. As for bringing about a marriage, I would almost rather bring about a murder."

"Poor Esther!" said he gloomily. "She has been brought up among men, and is not used to harness. If things go wrong she will rebel, and a woman who rebels is lost."

"Esther has known too many good men ever to marry a bad one," she replied.

"I am not sure of that," he answered. "When I am out of the way she will feel lonely, and any man who wants her very much can probably get her. Joking apart, it is there I want your help. Keep an eye on her. Your principles will let you prevent a marriage, even though you are not allowed to make one."

"I hope she will not want my help in either way," said Mrs. Murray; "but if she does, I will remember what you say--though I would rather go out to service at five dollars a week than do this kind of work. Do you know that I have already a girl on my hands? Poor Catherine Brooke's daughter is coming to-morrow from Colorado to be under my care for the next few months till she is of age. She never has been to the East, and I expect to have my hands full."

"If I had known it," said he, "I think I would have selected some wiser woman to look after Esther."

"You are too encouraging," replied Mrs. Murray. "If I talk longer with you I shall have a crying fit. Suppose we change the subject and amuse ourselves in a cheerfuller way."

They finished their drive talking of less personal matters, but Mrs. Murray, after leaving her brother-in-law at his house, went back to her own with spirits depressed to a point as low as any woman past fifty cares to enjoy. She had reason to know that Mr. Dudley was not mistaken about his symptoms, and that not many months could pass before that must happen which he foresaw. He could find some relief in talking and even in jesting about it, but she could only with difficulty keep herself from an outburst of grief. She had every reason to feel keenly. To lose one's oldest friends is a trial that human nature never accustoms itself to bear with satisfaction, even when the loss does not double one's responsibilities; but in this case Mrs. Murray, as she grew old, saw her niece Esther about to come on her hands at the same time when a wild girl from the prairie was on the road to her very door, and she had no sufficient authority to control either of them. For a woman without children of her own, to act this part of matron to an extemporized girls' college might be praise-worthy, but could not bring repose of mind or body.

Mrs. Murray was still wider awake to this truth when she went the next day to the Grand Central Station to wait for the arrival of her Colorado orphan. The Chicago express glided in as gracefully and silently as though it were in quite the best society, and had run a thousand miles or so only for gentle exercise before dining at Delmonico's and passing an evening at the opera. Among the crowd of passengers who passed out were several women whose appearance gave Mrs. Murray a pang of fear, but at length she caught sight of one who pleased her fastidious eye. "I hope it is she," broke from her lips as the girl came towards her, and a moment later her hope was gratified. She drew a breath of relief that made her light-hearted. Whatever faults the girl might have, want of charm was not among them. As she raised her veil, the engine-stoker, leaning from his engine above them, nodded approval. In spite of dust and cinders, the fatigue and exposure of two thousand miles or so of travel, the girl was fresh as a summer morning, and her complexion was like the petals of a sweetbrier rose. Her dark blue woollen dress, evidently made by herself, soothed Mrs. Murray's anxieties more completely than though it had come by the last steamer from the best modiste in Paris.

"Is it possible you have come all the way alone?" she asked, looking about with lurking suspicion of possible lovers still to be revealed.

"Only from Chicago," answered Catherine; "I stopped awhile there to rest, but I had friends to take care of me."

"And you were not homesick or lonely?"

"No! I made friends on the cars. I have been taking care of a sick lady and her three children, who are all on their way to Europe, and wanted to pay my expenses if I would go with them."

"I don't wonder!" said Mrs. Murray with an unusual burst of sympathy.

No sooner had they fairly reached the house than Esther came to see the stranger and found her aunt in high spirits. "She is as natural and sweet as a flower," said Mrs. Murray. "To be sure she has a few Western tricks; she says she stopped awhile at Chicago, and that she has a raft of things in her trunks, and she asks haeow, and says aeout; but so do half the girls in New York, and I will break her of it in a week so that you will never know she was not educated in Boston and finished in Europe. I was terribly afraid she would wear a linen duster and water-waves."

Catherine became a favorite on the spot. No one could resist her hazel eyes and the curve of her neck, or her pure complexion which had the transparency of a Colorado sunrise. Her good nature was inexhaustible, and she occasionally developed a touch of sentiment which made Mr. Murray assert that she was the most dangerous coquette within his experience. Mr. Murray, who had a sound though uncultivated taste for pretty girls, succumbed to her charms, while George Strong, whose good nature was very like her own, never tired of drawing her out and enjoying her comments on the new life about her.

"What kind of a revolver do you carry?" asked George, gravely, at his first interview with her; "do you like yours heavy, or say a 32 ball?"

"Don't mind him, Catherine," said Mrs. Murray; "he is always making poor jokes."

"Oh, but I'm not strong enough to use heavy shooting-irons," replied Catherine quite seriously. "I had a couple of light ones in my room at home, but father told me I could never hurt any thing with them, and I never did."

"Always missed your man?" asked George.

"I never fired at a man but once. One night I took one of our herders for a thief and shot at him, but I missed, and just got laughed at for a week. That was before we moved down to Denver, where we don't use pistols much."

Strong felt a little doubt whether she was making fun of him or he of her, and she never left him in perfect security on this point.

"What is your name in Sioux, Catherine," he would ask; "Laughing Strawberry, I suppose, or Jumping Turtle?"

"No!" she answered. "I have a very pretty name in Sioux. They call me the Sage Hen, because I am so quiet. I like it much better than my own name."

Strong was beaten at this game. She capped all his questions for him with an air of such good faith as made him helpless. Whether it were real or assumed, he could not make up his mind. He took a great fancy to the Sage Hen, while she in her turn took a violent liking for Esther, as the extremest contrast to herself. When Esther realized that this product of Colorado was likely to be on her hands for several hours every day, she felt less amused than either Strong or Mr. Murray, for Miss Brooke's conversation, though entertaining as far as it went, had not the charm of variety. It was not long before her visits to Esther's studio became so frequent and so exhausting that Esther became desperate and felt that some relief must at any cost be found. The poor little prairie flower found New York at first exciting; she felt shy and awkward among the swarms of strange people to whose houses Mrs. Murray soon began to take her by way of breaking her in at once to the manners of New York society; and whenever she could escape, she fled to Esther and her quiet studio, with the feelings of a bird to its nest. The only drawback to her pleasure there was that she had nothing to do; her reading seemed to have been entirely in books of a severely moral caste, and in consequence she could not be induced to open so much as a magazine. She preferred to chatter about herself and the people she met. Before a week had passed Esther felt that something must be done to lighten this burden, and it was then that, as we shall see, Mr. Hazard suggested her using Catherine for a model. The idea might not have been so easily accepted under other circumstances, but it seemed for the moment a brilliant one.

As Wharton had said of Esther, she was but a second-rate amateur. Whether there was a living artist whom Wharton would have classed higher than a first-rate amateur is doubtful. On his scale to be second-rate was a fair showing. Esther had studied under good masters both abroad and at home. She had not the patience to be thorough, but who had? She asked this question of Mr. Wharton when he attacked her for bad drawing, and Wharton's answer left on her mind the impression that he was himself the only thorough artist in the world; yet others with whom she talked hinted much the same thing of themselves. Esther at all events painted many canvases and panels, good or bad, some of which had been exhibited and had even been sold, more perhaps owing to some trick of the imagination which she had put into them than to their technical merit. Yet into one work she had put her whole soul, and with success. This was a portrait of her father, which that severe critic liked well enough to hang on the wall of his library, and which was admitted to have merits even by Wharton, though he said that its unusual and rather masculine firmness of handling was due to the subject and could never be repeated.

Catherine was charmed to sit for her portrait. It was touching to see the superstitious reverence with which this prairie child kneeled before whatever she supposed to be learned or artistic. She took it for granted that Esther's painting was wonderful; her only difficulty was to understand how a man so trivial as George Strong, could be a serious professor, in a real university. She thought that Strong's taste for bric-a-brac was another of his jokes. He tried to educate her, and had almost succeeded when, in producing his last and most perfect bit of Japanese lacquer, he said: "This piece, Catherine, is too pure for man. We pray to it." Catherine sat as serious as eternity, but she believed in her heart that he was making fun of her.

In this atmosphere, to sit for her portrait was happiness, because it made her a part of her society. Esther was surprised to find what a difficult model she was, with liquid reflections of eyes, hair and skin that would have puzzled Correggio. Of course she was to be painted as the Sage Hen. George sent for sage brush, and got a stuffed sage hen, and photographs of sage-plains, to give Esther the local color for her picture.

Chapter III

ONCE a week, if she could, Esther passed an hour or two with the children at the hospital. This building had accommodations for some twenty-five or thirty small patients, and as it was a private affair, the ladies managed it to please themselves. The children were given all the sunlight that could be got into their rooms and all the toys and playthings they could profitably destroy. As the doctors said that, with most of them, amusement was all they would ever get out of life, an attempt was made to amuse them. One large room was fitted up for the purpose, and the result was so satisfactory that Esther got more pleasure out of it than the children did. Here a crowd of little invalids, playing on the yellow floor or lying on couches, were always waiting to be amused and longing to be noticed, and thought themselves ill-treated if at least one of the regular visitors did not appear every day to hear of their pains and pleasures. Esther's regular task was to tell them a story, and, learning from experience that she could double its effect by illustrating it, she was in the custom of drawing, as she went on, pictures of her kings and queens, fairies, monkeys and lions, with amiable manners and the best moral characters. Thus drawing as she talked, the story came on but slowly, and spread itself over weeks and months of time.

On this Saturday afternoon Esther was at her work in the play-room, surrounded by a dozen or more children, with a cripple, tortured by hip-disease, lying at her side and clinging to her skirt, while a proud princess, with red and white cheeks and voluminous robes, was making life bright with colored crayons and more highly colored adventures, when the door opened and Esther saw the Rev. Stephen Hazard, with her aunt, Mrs. Murray, on the threshold.

Mr. Hazard was not to blame if the scene before him made a sudden and sharp picture on his memory. The autumn sun was coming in at the windows; the room was warm and pleasant to look at; on a wide brick hearth, logs of hickory and oak were burning; two tall iron fire-dogs sat up there on their hind legs and roasted their backs, animals in which the children were expected to take living interest because they had large yellow glass eyes through which the fire sparkled; with this, a group of small invalids whose faces and figures were stamped with the marks of organic disease; and in the center--Esther!

Mr. Hazard had come here this afternoon partly because he thought it his duty, and partly because he wanted to create closer relations with a parishioner so likely to be useful as Mrs. Murray. He was miserable with a cold, and was weak with fatigue. His next sermon was turning out dull and disjointed. His building committee were interfering and quarreling with Wharton. A harsh north-west wind had set his teeth on edge and filled his eyes with dust. Rarely had he found himself in a less spiritual frame of mind than when he entered this room. The contrast was overwhelming. When Esther at first said quite decidedly that nothing would induce her to go on with her story, he felt at once that this was the only thing necessary to his comfort, and made so earnest an appeal that she was forced to relent, though rather ungraciously, with a laughing notice that he must listen very patiently to her sermon as she had listened to his. The half hour which he now passed among kings and queens in tropical islands and cocoanut groves, with giants and talking monkeys, was one of peace and pleasure. He drew so good a monkey on a cocoanut tree that the children shouted with delight, and Esther complained that his competition would ruin her market. She rose at last to go, telling him that she was sorry to seem so harsh, but had she known that his pictures and stories were so much better than hers, she would never have voted to make him a visitor.

Mr. Hazard was flattered. He naturally supposed that a woman must have some fine quality if she could interest Wharton and Strong, two men utterly different in character, and at the same time amuse suffering children, and drag his own mind out of its deepest discouragement, without show of effort or consciousness of charm. In this atmosphere of charity, where all faiths were alike and all professions joined hands, the church and the world became one, and Esther was the best of allies; while to her eyes Mr. Hazard seemed a man of the world, with a talent for drawing and a quick imagination, gentle with children, pleasant with women, and fond of humor. She could not help thinking that if he would but tell pleasant stories in the pulpit, and illustrate them on a celestial blackboard such as Wharton might design, church would be an agreeable place to pass one's Sunday mornings in. As for him, when she went away with her aunt, he returned to his solitary dinner with a mind diverted from its current. He finished his sermon without an effort. He felt a sort of half-conscious hope that Esther would be again a listener, and that he might talk it over with her. The next morning he looked about the church and was disappointed at not seeing her there. This young man was used to flattery; he had been sickened with it, especially by the women of his congregation; he thought there was nothing of this nature against which he was not proof; yet he resented Esther Dudley's neglect to flatter him by coming to his sermon. Her absence was a hint that at least one of his congregation did not care to hear him preach a second time.

Piqued at this indifference to his eloquence and earnestness he went the next afternoon, according to his agreement, to Strong's rooms, knowing that Miss Dudley was to be there, and determined to win her over. The little family party which Strong had got together was intended more for this purpose than for any other, and Strong, willing to do what he could to smooth his friend's path, was glad to throw him in contact with persons from whom he could expect something besides flattery. Strong never conceived it possible that Hazard could influence them, but he thought their influence likely to be serious upon Hazard. He underrated his friend's force of character.

His eyes were soon opened. Catherine Brooke made her first appearance on this occasion, and was greatly excited at the idea of knowing people as intellectual as Mr. Hazard and Mr. Wharton. She thought them a sort of princes, and was still ignorant that such princes were as tyrannical as any in the Almanach de Gotha, and that those who submitted to them would suffer slavery. Her innocent eagerness to submit was charming, and the tyrants gloated over the fresh and radiant victim who was eager to be their slave. They lured her on, by assumed gentleness, in the path of bric-a-brac and sermons.

In her want of experience she appealed to Strong, who had not the air of being their accomplice, but seemed to her a rather weak-minded ally of her own. Strong had seated her by the window, and was teaching her to admire his collections, while Wharton and Hazard were talking with the rest of the party on the other side of the room.

"What kind of an artist is Mr. Wharton?" asked Catherine.

"A sort of superior house-painter," replied Strong. "He sometimes does glazing."

"Nonsense!" said Catherine contemptuously. "I know all about him. Esther has told me. I want to know how good an artist he is. What would they think of him in Paris?"

"That would depend on whether they owned any of his pictures," persisted Strong. "I think he might be worse. But then I have one of his paintings, and am waiting to sell it when the market price gets well up. Do you see it? The one over my desk in the corner. How do you like it?"

"Why does he make it so dark and dismal?" asked Catherine. "I can't make it out."

"That is the charm," he replied. "I never could make it out myself; let's ask him;" and he called across the room: "Wharton, will you explain to Miss Brooke what your picture is about? She wants to know, and you are the only man who can tell her."

Wharton in his grave way came over to them, and first looking sadly at Miss Brooke, then at the picture, said at length, as though to himself: "I thought it was good when I did it. I think it is pretty good now. What criticism do you make, Miss Brooke?"

Catherine was in mortal terror, but stood her ground like a heroine. "I said it seemed to me dark, Mr. Wharton, and I asked why you made it so."

Wharton looked again at the picture and meditated over it. Then he said: "Do you think it would be improved by being lighter?"

Although Catherine pleaded guilty to this shocking heresy, she did it with so much innocence of manner that, in a few minutes, Wharton was captured by her sweet face, and tried to make her understand his theory that the merit of a painting was not so much in what it explained as in what it suggested. Comments from the by-standers interfered with his success. Hazard especially perplexed Catherine's struggling attention by making fun of Wharton's lecture.

"Your idea of a picture," said he, "must seem to Miss Brooke like my Cincinnati parishioner's idea of a corn-field. I was one day admiring his field of Indian corn, which stretched out into the distance like Lake Erie in a yellow sunset, when the owner, looking at his harvest as solemnly as Wharton is looking at his picture, said that what he liked most was the hogs he could see out of it."

"Well," said Wharton, "the Dutch made a good school out of men like him. Art is equal to any thing. I will paint his hogs for him, slaughtered and hung up by the hind legs, and if I know how to paint, I can put his corn-field into them, like Ostade, and make the butchers glow with emotion."

"Don't believe him, Miss Brooke," said Hazard. "He wants you to do his own work, and if you give in to him you are lost. He covers a canvas with paint and then asks you to put yourself into it. He might as well hold up a looking-glass to you. Any man can paint a beautiful picture if he could persuade Miss Brooke to see herself in it."

"What a pretty compliment," said Esther. "It is more flattering than the picture."

"You can prove its truth, Miss Dudley," said Hazard. "It is easy to show that I am right. Paint Miss Brooke yourself! Give to her the soul of the Colorado plains! Show that beauty of subject is the right ideal! You will annihilate Wharton and do an immortal work."

Hazard's knack of fixing an influence wherever he went had long been the wonder of Strong, but had never surprised or amused him more than now, when he saw Esther, after a moment's hesitation, accept this idea, and begin to discuss with Hazard the pose and surroundings which were to give Catherine Brooke's picture the soul of the Colorado plains. Hazard drew well and had studied art more carefully than most men. He used to say that if he had not a special mission for the church, as a matter of personal taste he should have preferred the studio. He not only got at once into intimate relations with Esther and Catherine, but he established a sort of title in Esther's proposed portrait. Strong laughed to himself at seeing that even Mr. Dudley, who disliked the clergy more than any other form of virtue, was destined to fall a victim to Hazard's tact.

When the clergyman walked away from Strong's rooms that afternoon, he felt, although even to himself he would not have confessed it, a little elated. Instinct has more to do than vanity with such weaknesses, and Hazard's instinct told him that his success, to be lasting, depended largely on overcoming the indifference of people like the Dudleys. If he could not draw to himself and his church the men and women who were strong enough to have opinions of their own, it was small triumph to draw a procession of followers from a class who took their opinions, like their jewelry, machine-made. He felt that he must get a hold on the rebellious age, and that it would not prove rebellious to him. He meant that Miss Dudley should come regularly to church, and on his success in bringing her there, he was half-ready to stake the chances of his mission in life.

So Catherine's portrait was begun at once, when Catherine herself had been barely a week in New York. To please Esther, Mr. Dudley had built for her a studio at the top of his house, which she had fitted up in the style affected by painters, filling it with the regular supply of eastern stuffs, porcelains, and even the weapons which Damascus has the credit of producing; one or two ivory carvings, especially a small Italian crucifix; a lay figure; some Japanese screens, and eastern rugs. Her studio differed little from others, unless that it was cleaner than most; and it contained the usual array of misshapen sketches pinned against the wall, and of spoiled canvases leaning against each other in corners as though they were wall flower beauties pouting at neglect.

Here Catherine Brooke was now enthroned as the light of the prairie, and day after day for three weeks, Esther labored over the portrait with as much perseverance as though Hazard were right in promising that it should make her immortal. The last days of November and the first of December are the best in the year for work, and Esther worked with an energy that surprised her. She wanted to extort praise from Mr. Wharton, and even felt a slight shade of responsibility towards Mr. Hazard. At first no one was to be admitted to see it while in progress; then an exception was made for Strong and Hazard who came to the house one evening, and in a moment of expansiveness were told that they would be admitted to the studio. They came, and Esther found Mr. Hazard's suggestions so useful that she could not again shut him out. In return she was shamed into going to church with her aunt the following Sunday, where she heard Mr. Hazard preach again. She did not enjoy it, and did not think it necessary to repeat the compliment. "One should not know clergymen," she said in excuse to her father for not liking the sermon; "there is no harm in knowing an actress or opera-singer, but religion is a serious thing." Mr. Hazard did not know how mere a piece of civility her attendance was; he saw only that she was present, that his audience was larger and his success more assured than ever. With this he was well satisfied, and, as he had been used in life always to have his own way, he took it for granted that in this instance he had got it.

The portrait of course did not satisfy Esther. Do what she would, Catherine's features and complexion defied modeling and made the artificial colors seem hard and coarse. The best she could paint was not far from down-right failure. She felt the danger and called Mr. Hazard to her aid. Hazard suggested alterations, and insisted much on what he was pleased to call "values," which were not the values Esther had given. With his help the picture became respectable, as pictures go, although it would not have been with impunity that Tintoret himself had tried to paint the soul of the prairie.

Esther, like most women, was timid, and wanted to be told when she could be bold with perfect safety, while Hazard's grasp of all subjects, though feminine in appearance, was masculine and persistent in reality. To be steadily strong was not in Esther's nature. She was audacious only by starts, and recoiled from her own audacity. Before long, Hazard began to dominate her will. She felt a little uneasy until he had seen and approved her work. More than once he disapproved, and then she had to do it over again. She began at length to be conscious of this impalpable tyranny, and submitted to it only because she felt her own dependence and knew that in a few days more she should be free. If he had been clerical or dogmatic, she might have resented it and the charm would have broken to pieces on the spot, but he was for the time a painter like herself, as much interested in the art, and caring for nothing else.

Towards Christmas the great work was finished, and the same party that had met a month before at Strong's rooms, came together again in Esther's studio to sit upon and judge the portrait they had suggested. Mr. Dudley, with some effort, climbed up from his library; Mrs. Murray again acted as chaperon, and even Mr. Murray, whose fancy for pictures was his only known weakness, came to see what Esther had made of Catherine. The portrait was placed in a light that showed all its best points and concealed as far as possible all its weak ones; and Esther herself poured out tea for the connoisseurs.

To disapprove in such a company was not easy, but Wharton was equal to the task. He never compromised his convictions on such matters even to please his hosts, and in consequence had given offense to most of the picture-owners in the city of New York. He showed little mercy now to Esther, and perhaps his attack might have reduced her courage to despair, had she not found a champion who took her defense wholly on his own shoulders. It happened that Wharton attacked parts of the treatment for which Hazard was responsible, and when Hazard stepped into the lists, avowing that he had advised the work and believed it to be good, Esther was able to retire from the conflict and to leave the two men fighting a pitched battle over the principles of art. Hazard defended and justified every portion of the painting with a vigor and resource quite beyond Esther's means, and such as earned her lively gratitude. When he had reduced Wharton to silence, which was not a difficult task, for Wharton was a poor hand at dispute or argument, and felt rather than talked, Mr. Hazard turned to Esther who gave him a look of gratitude such as she had rarely conferred on any of his sex.

"I think we have ground him to powder at last," said Hazard with his boyish laugh of delight.

"I never knew before what it was to have a defender," said she simply.

Meanwhile Strong, who thought this battle no affair of his, was amusing himself as usual by chaffing Catherine. "I have told my colleague, who professes languages," said he, "that I have a young Sioux in the city, and he is making notes for future conversation with you."

"What will he talk about," asked Catherine; "are all professors as foolish as you?"

"He will be light and airy with you. He asked me what gens you belonged to. I told him I guessed it was the grouse gens. He said he had not been aware that such a totem existed among the Sioux. I replied that, so far as I could ascertain, you were the only surviving member of your family."

"Well, and what am I to say?" asked Catherine.

"Tell him that the Rocky Mountains make it their only business to echo his name," said Strong. "Have you an Indian grandmother?"

"No, but perhaps I could lariat an old aunt for him, if he will like me better for it."

"Aunt will do," said Strong. "Address the old gentleman in Sioux, and call him the 'dove with spectacles.' It will please his soft old heart, and he will take off his spectacles and fall in love with you. There is nothing so frivolous as learning; nothing else knows enough."

"I like him already," said Catherine. "A professor with spectacles is worth more than a Sioux warrior. I will go with him."

"Don't be in a hurry," replied Strong; "it will come to about the same thing in the end. My colleague will only want your head to dry and stuff for his collection."

"If I were a girl again," said Mrs. Murray, who was listening to their conversation, "I would much rather a man should ask for my head than my heart."

"That is what is the matter with all of you," said Strong. "There are Wharton and Esther at it again, quarreling about Catherine's head. Every body disputes about her head, and I am the only one who goes for her heart."

"Mr. Wharton is so stern," pleaded Esther in defense against the charge of quarreling. "A hundred times he has told me that I can't draw; he should have made me learn when he undertook to teach me."

"You might learn more easily now, if you would be patient about it," said Wharton. "You have too much quickness and not enough knowledge."

"I think Mr. Hazard turns his compliments better than you," said Esther. "After one of your speeches I have to catch my breath and think what it means."

"I mean that you ought to be a professional," replied Wharton.

"But if I were able to be a professional, do you think I would be an amateur?" asked Esther. "No! I would decorate a church."

"If that is all your ambition, do it now!" said Wharton. "Come and help me to finish St. John's. I have half a dozen workmen there who are certainly not so good as you."

"What will you give me to do?" asked she.

"I will engage you to paint, under my direction, a large female figure on the transept wall. There are four vacant spaces for which I have made only rough drawings, and you can try your hand on whichever you prefer. You shall be paid like the other artists, and you will find some other women employed there, to keep you company."

"Let me choose the subject," said Mr. Hazard. "I think I have a voice in the matter."

"That depends on your choice," replied Wharton.

"It must be St. Cecilia, of course," said Hazard; "and Miss Brooke must sit again as model."

"Could you not sit yourself as St. George on the dragon?" asked Strong. "I have just received a tertiary dragon from the plains, which I should like to see properly used in the interests of the church."

"Catherine is a better model," answered Esther.

"You've not yet seen my dragon. Let me bring him round to you. With Hazard on his back, he would fly away with you all into the stars."

"There are dragons enough at St. John's," answered Hazard. "I will ride on none of them."

"You've no sense of the highest art," said Strong. "Science alone is truth. You are throwing away your last chance to reconcile science and religion."

So, after much discussion, it was at last decided that Esther Dudley should begin work at St. John's as a professional decorator under Mr. Wharton's eye, and that her first task should be to paint a standing figure of St. Cecilia, some eight or ten feet high, on the wall of the north transept.

Chapter IV

ST. John's church was a pleasant spot for such work. The north transept, high up towards the vault of the roof, was still occupied by a wide scaffold which shut in the painters and shut out the curious, and ran the whole length of its three sides, being open towards the body of the church. When Esther came to inspect her field of labor, she found herself obliged to choose between a space where her painting would be conspicuous from below, and one where, except in certain unusual lights, it could hardly be seen at all. Partly out of delicacy, that she might not seem to crowd Wharton's own work into the darkness; partly out of pure diffidence, Esther chose the least conspicuous space, and there a sort of studio was railed off for her, breast high, within which she was mistress. Wharton, when painting, was at this time engaged at some distance, but on the same scaffolding, near the nave.

The great church was silent with the echoing silence which is audible. Except for a call from workmen below to those at work above, or for the murmur of the painters as they chatted in intervals of rest, or for occasional hammering, which echoed in hollow reverberations, no sound disturbed repose. Here one felt the meaning of retreat and self-absorption, the dignity of silence which respected itself; the presence which was not to be touched or seen. To a simple-minded child like Catherine Brooke, the first effect was as impressive as though she were in the church of St. Mark's. She was overwhelmed by the space and silence, the color and form; and as she came close to Wharton's four great figures of the evangelists and saw how coarsely they were painted, and looked sheer down from them upon the distant church-floor, she thought herself in an older world, and would hardly have felt surprised at finding herself turned into an Italian peasant-girl, and at seeing Michael Angelo and Raphael, instead of Wharton and Esther, walk in at the side door, and proceed to paint her in celestial grandeur and beauty, as the new Madonna of the prairie, over the high altar.

This humility lasted several minutes. Then after glancing steadfastly at Wharton's figure of John of Patmos which stood next to that which Esther was to paint, Catherine suddenly broke out:

"Shade of Columbus! You are not going to make me look like that?"

"I suppose I must," replied Esther, mischievously.

"Lean and dingy, in a faded brown blanket?" asked Catherine in evident anguish.

"So Mr. Wharton says," answered Esther, unrelentingly.

"Not if I'm there," rejoined Catherine, this time with an air of calm decision. "I'm no such ornery saint as that."

Henceforth she applied all her energies and feminine charms to the task of preventing this disaster, and her first effort was to make a conquest of Wharton. Esther stood in fear of the painter, who was apt to be too earnest to measure his words with great care. He praised little and found fault much. He broke out in rage with all work that seemed to him weak or sentimental. He required Esther to make her design on the spot that he might see moment by moment what it was coming to, and half a dozen times he condemned it and obliged her to begin anew. Almost every day occurred some scene of discouragement which made Esther almost regret that she had undertaken a task so hard.

Catherine, being encouraged by the idea that Esther was partly struggling for her sake, often undertook to join in the battle and sometimes got roughly handled for her boldness.

"Why can't you let her go her own way, Mr. Wharton, and see what she means to do?" asked Catherine one morning, after a week of unprofitable labor.

"Because she does not come here to go her own way, Miss Brooke, but to go the right way."

"But don't you see that she is a woman, and you are trying to make a man of her?"

"An artist must be man, woman and demi-god," replied Wharton sternly.

"You want me to be Michael Angelo," said Esther, "and I hate him. I don't want to draw as badly as he did."

Wharton gave a little snort of wrath: "I want you to be above your subject, whatever it is. Don't you see? You are trying to keep down on a level with it. That is not the path to Paradise. Put heaven in Miss Brooke's eyes! Heaven is not there now; only earth. She is a flower, if you like. You are the real saint. It is your own paradise that St. Cecilia is singing about. I want to make St. Cecilia glow with your soul, not with Miss Brooke's. Miss Brooke has got no soul yet."

"Neither have I," groaned Esther, making up a little face at Wharton's vehemence.

"No," said Wharton, seized with a gravity as sudden as his outbreak, "I suppose not. A soul is like a bird, and needs a sharp tap on its shell to open it. Never mind! One who has as much feeling for art as you have, must have soul some where."

This sort of lecture might be well enough for Esther, if she had the ability to profit by it, but Catherine had no mind to be thus treated as though she were an early Christian lay-figure. She flushed at hearing herself coolly flung aside like common clay, and her exquisite eyes half filled with tears as she broke out:

"I believe you think I'm a beetle because I come from Colorado! Why may I not have a soul as well as you?"

Wharton started at this burst of feeling; he felt as though he had really cracked the egg-shell of what he called a soul, in the wrong person; but he was not to be diverted from his lecture. "There, Miss Dudley," he said, "look at her now!" Then, catching a crayon, he continued: "Wait! Let me try it myself!" and began rapidly to draw the girl's features. Quite upset by this unexpected recoil of her attack, Catherine would have liked to escape, but the painter, when the fit was on him, became very imperious, and she dared not oppose his will. When at length he finished his sketch, he had the civility to beg her pardon.

"This is a man's work," said Esther, studying his drawing. "No woman would ever have done it. I don't like it. I prefer her as she is and as I made her."

Wharton himself seemed to be not perfectly satisfied with his own success, for he made no answer to Esther's criticism, and after one glance at his sketch, relapsed into moody silence. Perhaps he felt that what he had drawn was not a St. Cecilia at all, and still less a Catherine Brooke. He had narrowed the face, deepened its lines, made the eyes much stronger and darker, and added at least ten years to Catherine's age, in order to give an expression of passion subsided and heaven attained.

"You have reached Nirvana," said Esther to Catherine, still studying the sketch.

"What is Nirvana?" asked Catherine.

"Ask Mr. Wharton. He has put you there."

"Nirvana is what I mean by Paradise," replied Wharton slowly. "It is eternal life, which, my poet says, consists in seeing God."

"I would not like to look like that," said Catherine in an awe-struck tone. "Do you think this picture will ever be like me?"

"The gods forbid!" said the painter uneasily.

Catherine, who could not take her eyes from this revelation of the possible mysteries in her own existence, mysteries which for the first time seemed to have come so near as to over-shadow her face, now suddenly turned to Wharton and said with irresistible simplicity:

"Mr. Wharton, will you let me have it? I have no money. Will you give it to me?"

"You could not buy it. I will give it to you on one condition," replied Wharton.

"Don't make it a hard one."

"You shall forget that I said you had no soul."

"Oh!" said Catherine greatly relieved; "if I have one, you were the first to see it."

She carried the sketch away with her, nor has any one caught sight of it since she rolled it up. She refused to show it or talk of it, until even Strong was forced to drop the subject, and leave her to dream in peace of the romance that could give such a light to her eyes.

Strong was one of the few persons allowed to climb up to their perch and see their work. When he next came, Esther told him of Wharton's lecture, and of Catherine's sudden rebellion. Delighted with this new flight of his prairie bird, Strong declared that as they were all bent on taking likenesses of Catherine, he would like to try his own hand at it, and show them how an American Saint ought to look when seen by the light of science. He then set to work with Esther's pencils, and drew a portrait of Catherine under the figure of a large Colorado beetle, with wings extended. When it was done he pinned it against the wall.

"Now, Esther!" said he. "Take my advice. No one wants European saints over here; they are only clerical bric-a-brac, and what little meaning they ever had is not worth now a tolerable Japanese teapot; but here is a national saint that every one knows; not an American citizen can come into your church from Salt Lake City to Nantucket, who will not say that this is the church for his money; he will believe in your saints, for he knows them. Paint her so!"

"Very well!" said Catherine. "If Mr. Wharton will consent, I have no objection."

Wharton took it with his usual seriousness. "I believe you are right," said he sadly. "I feel more and more that our work is thrown away. If Hazard and the committee will consent, Miss Dudley shall paint what she likes for all me."

No one dared carry die joke so far as to ask Mr. Hazard's consent to canonize this American saint, and Strong after finishing his sketch, and labelling it: "Sta. Catarina 10-Lineata (Colorado)," gave it to Catherine as a companion to Wharton's. For some time she was called the beetle. Wharton's conscience seemed to smite him for his rudeness, and Catherine was promoted to the position of favorite. While Esther toiled over the tiresome draperies of her picture, Catherine would wander off with Wharton on his tours of inspection; she listened to all the discussions, and picked up the meaning of his orders and criticisms; in a short time she began to maintain opinions of her own. Wharton liked to have her near him, and came to get her when she failed to appear at his rounds. They became confidential and sympathetic.

"Are you never homesick for your prairie?" he asked one day.

"Not a bit!" she answered. "I like the East. What is the use of having a world to one's self?"

"What is the use of any thing?" asked Wharton.

"I give it up," she replied. "Does art say that a woman is no use?"

"I know of nothing useful in life," said he, "except what is beautiful or creates beauty. You are beautiful, and ought to be most so on your prairie."

"Am I really beautiful?" asked Catherine with much animation. "No one ever told me so before."

This was coquetry. The young person had often heard of the fact, and, even had she not, her glass told her of it several times a day. She meant only that this was the first time the fact came home to her as a new and exquisite sensation.

"You have the charm of the Colorado hills, and plains," said he. "But you won't keep it here. You will become self-conscious, and self-consciousness is worse than ugliness."

"Nonsense!" said Catherine boldly. "I know more art than you, if that is your notion. Do you suppose girls are so savage in Denver as not to know when they are pretty? Why, the birds are self-conscious! So are horses! So are antelopes! I have seen them often showing off their beauties like New York women, and they are never so pretty as then."

"Don't try it," said he. "If you do, I shall warn you. Tell me, do you think my figure of St. Paul here self-conscious? I lie awake nights for fear I have made him so."

Catherine looked long at the figure and then shook her head. "I could tell you if it were a woman," she said. "All women are more or less alike; but men are quite different, and even the silly ones may have brains somewhere. How can I tell?"

"A grain of self-consciousness would spoil him," said Wharton.

"Then men must be very different from women," she replied. "I will give you leave to paint me on every square inch of the church, walls and roof, and defy you to spoil any charm you think I have, if you will only not make me awkward or silly; and you may make me as self-conscious as Esther's St. Cecilia there, only she calls it modesty."

Catherine was so pulled about and put to such practical uses in art as to learn something by her own weary labors. A quick girl soon picks up ideas when she hears clever men talking about matters which they understand. Esther began to feel a little nervous. Catherine took so kindly to every thing romantic that Wharton began to get power over her. He had a queer imagination of his own, which she could not understand, but which had a sort of fascination for her. She ran errands for him, and became a sort of celestial messenger about the church. As for Wharton, he declared that she stood nearer nature than any woman he knew, and she was in sympathy with his highest emotions. He let her ask innumerable questions, which he answered or not, as happened to suit his mood. He paid no attention to Esther's remonstrances at being deprived of her model, but whenever he wanted Catherine for any purpose, he sent for her, and left Esther to her own resources. Catherine had her own reasons for being docile and for keeping him in good humor. She started with the idea that she did not intend to be painted, if she could help it, as a first century ascetic, without color, and clothed in a hair-cloth wrapper; and having once begun the attempt to carry her own object, she was drawn on without the power to stop.

Her intimacy with Wharton began to make Esther uneasy, so that one day, when Strong came up, and, missing Catherine, asked what had become of her, she consulted him on the subject.

"Catherine has gone off with Mr. Wharton to inspect," she said. "He comes for her or sends for her every day. What can I do about it?"

"Where is the harm?" asked Strong. "If she likes to pass an hour or two doing that sort of thing, I should think it was good for her."

"But suppose she takes a fancy to him?"

"Oh! No woman could marry Wharton," said Strong. "He would forget her too often, and she would lose patience with him before he thought of her again. Give her her head! He will teach her more that is worth her knowing than she would learn in a life-time in Aunt Sarah's parlor."

"I wish I could give her something else to amuse her."

"Well!" replied Strong. "We will invent something." Catherine returned a few minutes later, and he asked her how she got on with the task-master, and whether he had yet recovered her favor.

"Since the beetle turned on him," said Catherine, "we have got on like two little blind mice. He has been as kind to me as though I were his mother; but why is he so mysterious? He will not tell me his history."

"He is the same to us all," said Strong. "Some people think he is ashamed of his origin. He was picked out of the gutters of Cincinnati by some philanthropist and sent abroad for an education. The fact is that he cares no more about his origin than you do for being a Sioux Indian, but he had the misfortune to marry badly in Europe, and hates to talk of it."

"Then he has a wife already, when he is breaking my young heart?" exclaimed Catherine.

"I would like to calm your fears, my poor child," said Strong; "but the truth is that no one knows what has become of his wife. She may be alive, and she may be dead. Do you want me to find out?"

"I am dying to know," said Catherine; "but I will make him tell me all about it one of these days."

"Never!" replied Strong. "He lives only in his art since the collapse of his marriage. He eats and drinks paint."

"Does he really paint so very well?" asked Catherine thoughtfully. "Is he a great genius?"

"Young woman, we are all of us great geniuses. We never say so, because we are as modest as we are great, but just look into my book on fossil batrachians."

"I don't feel the least interest in you or your batrachiums; but I adore Mr. Wharton."

"What is the good of your adoring Wharton?" asked the professor. "Short's very good as far as he goes, but the real friend is Codlin, not Short."

"I shall hate you if you always make fun of me. What do you mean by your Codlins and Shorts?"

"Did you never read Dickens?" cried Strong.

"I never read a novel in my life, if that is what you are talking about," answered Catherine.

"Ho! Cousin Esther! The Sioux don't read Dickens. You should join the tribe."

"I always told you that sensible people never read," said Esther, hard at work on her painting. "Do you suppose St. Cecilia ever read Dickens or would have liked him if she had?"

"Perhaps not," said Strong. "I take very little stock in saints, and she strikes me as a little of a humbug, your Cecilia; but I would like to know what the effect of the 'Old Curiosity Shop' would be on a full-blooded Indian squaw. Catherine, will you try to read it if I bring you a copy here?"

"May I?" asked Catherine. "You know I was taught to believe that novels are sinful."

Strong stared at her a moment with surprise that any new trait in her could surprise him, and then went on solemnly: "Angel, you are many points too good for this wicked city. If you remain here unperverted, you will injure our trade. I must see to it that your moral tone is lowered. Will you read a novel of this person named Dickens if Mr. Hazard will permit you to do so in his church?"

"If Mr. Hazard says I must, I shall do so with pleasure," replied Catherine with her best company manners; and the Reverend Mr. Hazard, having been taken into Esther's confidence on the subject, decided, after reflection, that Miss Brooke's moral nature would not be hurt by reading Dickens under such circumstances; so the next day Catherine was plunged into a new world of imagination which so absorbed her thoughts that for the time Wharton himself seemed common-place. High on her scaffolding which looked sheer down into the empty, echoing church, with huge saints and evangelists staring at her from every side, and martyrs admiring each other's beatitude, Catherine, who was already half inclined to think life unreal, fell into a dream within a dream, and wondered which was untrue.

Esther's anxiety about Catherine was for the time put at rest by the professor's little maneuver, but she had some rather more serious cause for disquiet about herself, in regard to which she did not care to consult her cousin or any one else. Wharton and Strong were not the only men who undertook to enliven her path of professional labor. Every day at noon, the Reverend Stephen Hazard visited his church to see how Wharton was coming forward, and this clerical duty was not neglected after Esther joined the work-people. Much as Mr. Hazard had to do, and few men in New York were busier, he never forgot to look in for a moment on the artists, and Esther could not help noticing that this moment tended to lengthen. He had a way of joining Wharton and Catherine on their tour of inspection, and then bringing Catherine back to Esther's work-place, and sitting down for an instant to rest and look at the St. Cecilia. Time passed rapidly, and once or twice it had come over Esther's mind that, for a very busy man, Mr. Hazard seemed to waste a great deal of time. It grew to be a regular habit that between noon and one o'clock, Esther and Catherine entertained the clergyman of the parish.

The strain of standing in a pulpit is great. No human being ever yet constructed was strong enough to offer himself long as a light to humanity without showing the effect on his constitution. Buddhist saints stand for years silent, on one leg, or with arms raised above their heads, but the limbs shrivel, and the mind shrivels with the limbs. Christian saints have found it necessary from time to time to drop their arms and to walk on their legs, but they do it with a sort of apology or defiance, and sometimes do it, if they can, by stealth. One is a saint or one is not; every man can choose the career that suits him; but to be saint and sinner at the same time requires singular ingenuity. For this reason, wise clergymen, whose tastes, though in themselves innocent, may give scandal to others, enjoy their relaxation, so far as they can, in privacy. Mr. Hazard liked the society of clever men and agreeable women; he was bound to keep an eye on the progress of his own church; he stepped not an inch outside the range of his clerical duty and privilege; yet ill-natured persons, and there were such in his parish, might say that he was carrying on a secular flirtation in his own church under the pretense of doing his duty. Perhaps he felt the risk of running into this peril. He invited no public attention to the manner in which he passed this part of his time, and never alluded to the subject in other company.

To make his incessant attention still more necessary, it happened that Hazard's knowledge and his library were often drawn upon by Wharton and his workmen. Not only was he learned in all matters which pertained to church arrangement and decoration, but his collection of books on the subject was the best in New York, and his library touched the church wall. Wharton had a quantity of his books in constant use, and was incessantly sending to consult about points of doubt. Hazard was bent upon having every thing correct, and complained sadly when he found that his wishes were not regarded. He lectured Wharton on the subject of early Christian art until he saw that Wharton would no longer listen, and then he went off to Miss Dudley, and lectured her.

Esther was not a good subject for instruction of this sort. She cared little for what the early Christians believed, either in religion or art, and she remembered nothing at all of his deep instruction on the inferences to be drawn from the contents of crypts and catacombs. The more earnest he became, the less could she make out his meaning. She could not reconcile herself to draw the attenuated figures and haggard forms of the early martyrs merely because they suited the style of church decoration; and she could see no striking harmony of relation between these ill-looking beings and the Fifth Avenue audience to whom they were supposed to have some moral or sentimental meaning. After one or two hesitating attempts to argue this point, she saw that it was useless, and made up her mind that as a matter of ordinary good manners, the least she could do was to treat Mr. Hazard civilly in his own church, and listen with respect to his lectures on Christian art. She even did her best to obey his wishes in all respects in which she understood them, but here an unexpected and confusing play of cross-purposes came in to mislead her. Wharton suddenly found that Hazard let Miss Dudley have her own way to an extent permitted to no one else. Esther was not conscious that the expression of a feeling or a wish on her part carried any special weight, but there could be no doubt that if Miss Dudley seemed to want any thing very much, Mr. Hazard showed no sense of shame in suddenly forgetting his fixed theories and encouraging her to do what she pleased. This point was settled when she had been some ten days at work trying to satisfy Wharton's demands, which were also Mr. Hazard's, in regard to the character and expression of St. Cecilia. Catherine was so earnest not to be made repulsive, and Esther's own tastes lay so strongly in the same direction, that when it came to the point, she could not force herself to draw such a figure as was required; she held out with a sort of feminine sweetness such as cried aloud for discipline, and there was no doubt that Wharton was quite ready to inflict it. In spite of Catherine, and Esther too, he would have carried his point, had Esther not appealed to Mr. Hazard; but this strenuous purist, who had worried Wharton and the building committee with daily complaints that the character of their work wanted spiritual earnestness, now suddenly, at a word from Miss Dudley, turned about and encouraged her, against Wharton's orders, to paint a figure, which, if it could be seen, which was fortunately not the case, must seem to any one who cared for such matters, out of keeping with all the work which surrounded it.

"Do you know," said Esther to Mr. Hazard, "that Mr. Wharton insists on my painting Catherine as though she were forty years old and rheumatic?"

"I know," he replied, glancing timidly towards the procession of stern and elderly saints and martyrs, finished and unfinished, which seemed to bear up the church walls. "Do you think she would feel at home here if she were younger or prettier?"

"No! Honestly, I don't think she would," said Esther, becoming bold as he became timid. "I will paint Cecilia eighty years old, if Mr. Wharton wants her so. She will have lost her touch on the piano, and her voice will be cracked, but if you choose to set such an example to your choir, I will obey. But I can't ask Catherine to sit for such a figure. I will send out for some old woman, and draw from her."

"I can't spare Miss Brooke," said Hazard hastily. "The church needs her. Perhaps you can find some middle way with Wharton."

"No! If I am to paint her at all, I must paint her as she is. There is more that is angelic in her face now, if I could only catch it, than there is in all Mr. Wharton's figures put together, and if I am to commit sacrilege, I would rather be untrue to Mr. Wharton, than to her."

"I believe you are right, Miss Dudley. There *is* a little look of heaven in Miss Brooke's eyes. If you think you can put it into the St. Cecilia, why not try? If the experiment fails you can try again on another plan. After all, the drapery is the only part that needs to be very strictly in keeping."

Thus this despotic clergyman gave way and irritated Wharton, who, having promised to let him decide the dispute, was now suddenly overruled. He shrugged his shoulders and told Esther in private that he had struggled hard to get permission to do what she was doing, but only the sternest, strongest types would satisfy the church then. "It was all I could do to get them down to the thirteenth century," he said; "whenever I begged for beauty of form, they asked me whether I wanted the place to look like a theater."

"You know they're quite right," said Esther. "It has a terribly grotesque air of theater even now."

"It *is* a theater," growled Wharton. "That is what ails our religion. But it is not the fault of our art, and if you had come here a little earlier, I would have made one more attempt. I would like now, even as it is, to go back to the age of beauty, and put a Madonna in the heart of their church. The place has no heart."

"I never could have given you help enough for that, Mr. Wharton; but what does it matter about my poor Cecilia? She does no harm up here. No one can see her, and after all it is only her features that are modern!"

"No harm at all, but I wish I were a woman like you. Perhaps I could have my own way."

Esther liked to have her own way. She had the instinct of power, but not the love of responsibility, and now that she found herself allowed to violate Wharton's orders and derange his plans, she became alarmed, asked no more favors, stuck closely to her work, and kept Catherine always at her side. She even tried to return on her steps and follow Wharton's wishes, until she was stopped by Catherine's outcry. Then it appeared that Wharton had gone over to her side. Instead of supporting Esther in giving severity to the figure, he wanted it to be the closest possible likeness of Catherine herself. Esther began to think that men were excessively queer and variable; the more she tried to please them, the less she seemed to succeed; but Mr. Wharton certainly took more interest in the St. Cecilia as it advanced towards completion, although it was not in the least the kind of work which he liked or respected.

Mr. Hazard took not so much interest in the painting. His pleasure in visiting their gallery seemed to be of a different sort. As Esther learned to know him better, she found that he was suffering from over-work and responsibility, and that the painters' gallery was a sort of refuge, where he escaped from care, for an entire change of atmosphere and thought. In this light Esther found him a very charming fellow, especially when he was allowed to have his own way without question or argument. He talked well; drew well; wrote well, and in case of necessity could even sing fairly well. He had traveled far and wide, and had known many interesting people. He had a sense of humor, except where his church was concerned. He was well read, especially in a kind of literature of which Esther had heard nothing, the devotional writings of the church, and the poetry of religious expression. Esther liked to pick out plums of poetry, without having to search for them on her own account, and as Hazard liked to talk even better than she to listen, they babbled on pleasantly together while Catherine read novels which Hazard chose for her, and which he selected with the idea of carrying her into the life of the past. There was an atmosphere of romance about her novels, and not about the novels alone.

Chapter V

WHILE this ecclesiastical idyl was painting and singing itself in its own way, blind and deaf to the realities of life, this life moved on in its accustomed course undisturbed by idyls. The morning's task was always finished at one o'clock. At that hour, if the weather was fine, Mr. Dudley commonly stopped at the church door to take them away, and the rest of the day was given up to society. Esther and Catherine drove, made calls, dined out, went to balls, to the theater and opera, without interrupting their professional work. Under Mrs. Murray's potent influence, Catherine glided easily into the current of society and became popular without an effort. She soon had admirers. One young man, of an excellent and very old Dutch family, Mr. Rip Van Dam, took a marked fancy for her. Mr. Van Dam knew nothing of her, except that she was very pretty and came from Colorado where she had been brought up to like horses, and could ride almost any thing that would not buck its saddle off. This was quite enough for Mr. Van Dam whose taste for horses was more decided than for literature or art. He took Catherine to drive when the sleighing was good, and was flattered by her enthusiastic admiration of his beautiful pair of fast trotters. His confidence in her became boundless when he found that she could drive them quite as well as he. His success in winning her affections would have been greater if Catherine had not found his charms incessantly counteracted by the society of the older and more intelligent men, whom she never met at balls, but whom she saw every morning at the church, and whose tastes and talk struck her imagination. She liked Mr. Van Dam, but she laughed at him, which proved a thoughtless mind, for neither artists, clergymen nor professors were likely to marry her, as this young man might perhaps have done, under sufficient encouragement. When, towards the first of January, Catherine left Mrs. Murray, in order to stay with Esther, for greater convenience in the church work, Mr. Van Dam's attentions rather fell off. He was afraid of Esther, whom he insisted on regarding as clever, although Esther took much care never to laugh at him, for fear of doing mischief.

Catherine learned to play whist in order to amuse Mr. Dudley. They had small dinners, at which Hazard was sometimes present, and more often Strong, until he was obliged to go West to deliver a course of lectures at St. Louis. In spite of Mr. Dudley's supposed dislike for clergymen, he took kindly to Hazard and made no objection to his becoming a tame cat about the house. To make up a table at whist, Hazard did not refuse to take a hand; and said it was a part of his parochial duty. Mr. Dudley laughed and told him that if he performed the rest of his parochial duties equally ill, the parish should give him a year's leave of absence for purposes of study. Mr. Dudley disliked nothing so much as to be treated like an invalid, or to be serious, and Hazard gratified him by laughing at the doctors. They got on wonderfully well together, to the increasing amazement of Esther.

Card-playing and novel-reading were not the only cases in which Mr. Hazard took a liberal view of his functions. His theology belonged to the high-church school, and in the pulpit he made no compromise with the spirit of concession, but in all ordinary matters of indifference or of innocent pleasure he gave the rein to his instincts, and in regard to art he was so full of its relations with religion that he would admit of no divergence between the two. Art and religion might take great liberties with each other, and both be the better for it, as he thought.

His thirteenth-century ideas led him into a curious experiment which was quite in the thirteenth-century spirit. Catherine's insatiable spirit of coquetry was to blame, although it was not with him that she coquetted. Ready enough to try her youthful powers on most men, she had seemed to recognize by instinct that Mr. Hazard did not belong to her. Yet she could not rest satisfied without putting even him to some useful purpose of her own.

During Hazard's visits to the scaffold, he sometimes took up a pencil and drew. Once he drew a sketch of Wharton in the character of a monk with his brush and pallet in his hands. Catherine asked what connection there was between Mr. Wharton and a monastery.

"None!" replied Mr. Hazard; "but I like to think of church work as done by churchmen. In the old days he would have been a monk and would have painted himself among these figures on the walls."

Esther ventured to criticise Wharton's style; she thought it severe, monotonous, and sometimes strained.

"Wharton's real notion of art," said Hazard, "is a volcano. You may be a volcano at rest, or extinct, or in full eruption, but a volcano of some kind you have got to be. In one of his violent moods he once made me go over to Sicily with him, and dragged me to the top of Etna. It fascinated him, and I thought he meant to jump into it and pull me after him, but at that time he was a sort of used-up volcano himself."

"Then there is really something mysterious about his life?" asked Catherine.

"Only that he made a very unhappy marriage which he dislikes to think about," replied Hazard. "As an artist it did him good, but it ruined his peace and comfort, if he ever had any. He would never have made the mistake, if he had not been more ignorant of the world than any mortal that ever drew breath, but, as I was saying, a volcano was like a rattlesnake to him, and the woman he married was a volcano."

"What has become of her?" asked Esther.

"I have not dared to ask for years. No one seems to know whether she is living or dead."

"Did he leave her?"

"No; she left him. He was to the last fascinated by her, so much so that, after she left him, when I persuaded him to quit Paris, he insisted on going to Avignon and Vaucluse, because Petrarch had been under the same sort of fascination, and Wharton thought himself the only man in the world who could understand Petrarch. If you want to insult him and make him bitterly hate you, tell him that Laura was a married woman with a dozen children."

"Who was Laura?" asked Catherine; "and why should she not have a dozen children?"

"Laura was a beautiful girl with golden hair and a green dress whom Petrarch first saw in a church at Avignon," answered Hazard. "She was painted among the frescoes of the cathedral, as you are being painted now, Miss Brooke; and Petrarch wrote some hundreds of sonnets about her which Wharton undertook to translate, and made me help him. We were both poets then."

"I want to hear those sonnets," said Catherine, quite seriously, as though the likeness between herself and Laura had struck her as the most natural thing in the world. "Can you remember them?"

"I think I could. Don't find fault with me if you dislike the moral. I approve it because, like Petrarch, I am a bit of a churchman, but I don't know what you may think of a lover who begins by putting his mistress on the same footing with his deity and ends by groaning over the time he has thrown away on her."

"Not to her face?" said Esther.

"Worse! He saw her in church and wrote to her face something like this:

       'As sight of God is the eternal life,   Nor more we ask, nor more to wish we dare,   So, lady, sight of thee,'

and so on, or words to that effect. Yet after she was dead he said he had wasted his life in loving her. I remember the whole of the sonnet because it cost me two days' labor in the railway between Avignon and Nice. It runs like this:--

> 'For my lost life lamenting now I go,
>> Which I have placed in loving mortal thing,
>> Soaring to no high flight, although the wing
> Had strength to rise and loftier sweep to show.
> Oh! Thou that seest my mean life and low!
>> Invisible! Immortal! Heaven's king!
>> To this weak, pathless spirit, succor bring,
> And on its earthly faults thy grace bestow!
> That I, who lived in tempest and in fear,
>> May die in port and peace; and if it be
> That life was vain, at least let death be dear!
>> In these few days that yet remain to me,
> And in death's terrors, may thy hand be near!
>> Thou knowest that I have no hope but thee!'

In the Italian this is very great poetry, Miss Brooke, and if you don't think it so in my English, try and see if you can do better."

"Very well," said Catherine, coolly. "I've no doubt we can do it just as well as you and Mr. Wharton. Can't we, Esther?"

"You are impudent enough to make St. Cecilia blush," said Esther, who happened to be wondering whether she might dare to put a little blush into the cheeks of the figure on which she was painting. "You never read a word of Italian in your little life."

"No! But you have!" replied Catherine, as though this were final.

"The libretto of Lucia!" said Esther with scorn.

"No matter!" resumed Catherine. "Bring me the books, Mr. Hazard, and I will translate one of those sonnets if I have to shut up Esther in a dark closet."

"Catherine! Don't make me ridiculous!" said Esther; but Catherine was inspired by an idea, and would not be stopped.

"Bring me the volume now, Mr. Hazard! You shall have your sonnet for Sunday's sermon."

"Don't do it, Mr. Hazard!" exhorted Esther solemnly. "It is one of her Colorado jokes. She does not know what a sonnet is. She thinks it some kind of cattle-punching."

"If I do not give you that sonnet," cried Catherine, "I will give you leave to have me painted as much like an old skeleton as Mr. Wharton chooses."

"Done!" said Hazard, who regarded this as at least one point worth gaining. "You shall have the books. I want to see Wharton's triumph."

"But if I do poetry for you," continued Catherine, "you must do painting for me."

"Very well!" said Hazard. "What shall it be?"

"If I am Laura," said Catherine, "I must have a Petrarch. I want you to put him up here on the wall, looking at me, as he did in the church where he first saw me."

"But what will Wharton and the committee say?" replied Hazard, startled at so monstrous a demand.

"I don't believe Mr. Wharton will object," answered Catherine. "He will be flattered. Don't you see? He is to be Petrarch."

"Oh!" cried Hazard, with a stare. "Now I understand. You want me to paint Wharton as a scriptural character looking across to Miss Dudley's Cecilia."

"You are very slow!" said Catherine. "I think you might have seen it without making me tell you."

To a low-church evangelical parson this idea might have seemed inexpressibly shocking, but there was something in it which, after a moment's reflection, rather pleased Hazard. It was the sort of thing which the Florentines did, and there was hardly an early church in Italy about whose walls did not cling the colors of some such old union of art and friendship in the service of religion. Catherine's figure was already there. Why not place Wharton's by its side and honor the artist who had devoted so large a share of his life to the service of the church, with, it must be confessed, a very moderate share of worldly profit. The longer Hazard thought of it, the less he saw to oppose. His tastes were flattered by the idea of doing something with his own hand that should add to the character and meaning of the building. His imagination was so pleased with the notion that at last he gave his consent:--"Very well, Miss Brooke! I will draw a figure for this next vacant space, and carry it as far as I know how. If Wharton objects he can efface it. But Miss Dudley will have to finish it for me, for I can't paint, and Wharton would certainly stop me if I tried."

Although this pretty bargain which seemed so fair, really threw on Esther the whole burden of writing sonnets and painting portraits for the amusement of Catherine and Mr. Hazard, Catherine begged so hard that she at last consented to do her best, and her consent so much delighted Hazard that he instantly searched his books for a model to work from, and as soon as he found one to answer his purpose, he began with Esther's crayons to draw the cartoon of a large figure which was to preserve under the character of St. Luke the memory of Wharton's features. When Wharton came next to inspect Esther's work, he was told that Mr. Hazard wished to try his hand on designing a figure for the vacant space, and he criticised and corrected it as freely as the rest. For such a task Hazard was almost as competent as Wharton, from the moment the idea was once given, and in this dark corner it mattered little whether a conventional saint were more or less correct.

Meanwhile Catherine carried off a copy of Petrarch, and instantly turned it over to Esther, seeming to think it a matter of course that she should do so trifling a matter as a sonnet with ease. "It won't take you five minutes if you put your mind to it," she said. "You can do any thing you like, and any one could make a few rhymes." Esther, willing to please her, tried, and exhausted her patience on the first three lines. Then Catherine told the story to Mr. Dudley, who was so much amused by her ambition that he gave his active aid, and between them they succeeded in helping Esther to make out a sonnet which Mr. Dudley declared to be quite good enough for Hazard. This done, Esther refused to mix further in the matter, and made Catherine learn her verses by heart. The young woman found this no easy task, but when she thought herself perfect she told Mr. Hazard, as she would have told a schoolmaster, that she was ready with her sonnet.

"I have finished the sonnet, Mr. Hazard," she said one morning in a bashful voice, as though she were again at school.

"Where is it, Miss Brooke?"

Then Catherine, drawing herself up, with her hands behind her, began to recite:

"Oh, little bird! singing upon your way,
    Or mourning for your pleasant summer-tide,
    Seeing the night and winter at your side,
The joyous months behind, and sunny day!
If, as you know your own pathetic lay,
    You knew as well the sorrows that I hide,
    Nestling upon my breast, you would divide
Its weary woes, and lift their load away.
I know not that our shares would then be even,
    For she you mourn may yet make glad your sight,
While against me are banded death and heaven;
    But now the gloom of winter and of night
With thoughts of sweet and bitter years for leaven,
    Lends to my talk with you a sad delight."

Esther laughed till the tears rolled down her face at the droll effect of these tenderly sentimental verses in Catherine's mouth, but Hazard took it quite seriously and was so much delighted with Catherine's recitation that he insisted on her repeating it to Wharton, who took it even more seriously than he. Hazard knew that the verses were Esther's, and was not disposed to laugh at them. Wharton saw that Catherine came out with new beauties in every *role* she filled, and already wanted to use her as a model for some future frescoed Euterpe. Esther was driven to laugh alone.

Petrarch and Laura are dangerous subjects of study for young people in a church. Wharton and Hazard knew by heart scores of the sonnets, and were fond of repeating verses either in the original or in their own translations, and Esther soon picked up what they let fall, being quick at catching what was thrown to her. She caught verse after verse of Hazard's favorites, and sometimes he could hear her murmuring as she painted:

"Siccome eterna vita e veder dio,   Ne piu si brama, ne bramar piu lice;"

and at such moments he began to think that he was himself Petrarch, and that to repeat to his Laura the next two verses of the sonnet had become the destiny of his life.

So the weeks ran on until, after a month of hard work, the last days of January saw the two figures nearly completed. When in due time the meaning of St. Luke became evident, Esther and Catherine waited in fear to see how Wharton would take the liberty on which they had so rashly ventured. As the likeness came out more strongly, he stopped one morning before it, when Esther, after finishing her own task, was working on Mr. Hazard's design.

"By our lady of love!" said Wharton, with a start and a laugh; "now I see what mischief you three have been at!"

"The church would not have been complete without it," said Esther timidly.

For several minutes Wharton looked in silence at the St. Cecilia and at the figure which now seemed its companion; then he said, turning away: "I shall not be the first unworthy saint the church has canonized."

Esther drew a long breath of relief; Catherine started up, radiant with delight; and thus it happens that on the walls of St. John's, high above the world of vanities beneath them, Wharton stands, and will stand for ages, gazing at Catherine Brooke.

Now that the two saints were nearly finished, Esther became a little depressed. This church life, like a bit of religious Bohemianism and acted poetry, had amused her so greatly that she found her own small studio dull. She could no longer work there without missing the space, the echoes, the company, and above all, the sense of purpose, which she felt on her scaffolding. She complained to Wharton of her feminine want of motive in life.

"I wish I earned my living," she said. "You don't know what it is to work without an object."

"Much of the best work in the world," said he, "has been done with no motive of gain."

"Men can do so many things that women can't," said she. "Men like to work alone. Women cannot work without company. Do you like solitude?"

"I would like to own a private desert," he answered, "and live alone in the middle of it with lions and tigers to eat intruders."

"You need not go so far," said she. "Take my studio!"

"With you and Miss Brooke in the neighborhood? Never!"

"We will let you alone. In a week you will put your head out of the door and say: 'Please come and play jack-straws with me!'"

Catherine was not pleased at the thought that her usefulness was at an end. She had no longer a part to play unless it were that of duenna to Esther, and for this she was not so well fitted as she might have been, had providence thought proper to make her differently. Indeed, Esther's anxiety to do her duty as duenna to Catherine was becoming so sharp that it threatened to interfere with the pleasure of both. Catherine did her best to give her friend trouble.

"Please rub me all out, Mr. Wharton," said she; "and make Esther begin again. I am sure she will do it better the next time."

Wharton was quite ready to find an excuse for pleasing her. If it was at times a little annoying to have two women in his way whom he could not control as easily as ordinary work-people, he had become so used to the restraint as not to feel it often, and not to regard it much. Esther thought he need not distress himself by thinking that he regarded it at all. Had not Catherine been so anxious to appear as the most docile and obedient of hand-maids besides being the best-tempered of prairie creatures, she would long ago have resented his habit of first petting, then scolding, next ignoring, and again flattering her, as his mood happened to prompt. He was more respectful with Esther, and kept out of her way when he was moody, while she made it a rule never to leave her own place of work unless first invited, but Catherine, who was much by his side, got used to ill-treatment which she bore with angelic meekness. When she found herself left forgotten in a corner, or unanswered when she spoke, or unnoticed when she bade him good-morning, she consoled herself with reflecting that after every rudeness, Wharton's regard for her seemed to rise, and he took her more and more into his confidence with every new brutality.

"Some day he will drag you to the altar by the hair," said Esther; "and tell you that his happiness requires you to be his wife."

"I wish he would try," said Catherine with a little look of humor; "but he has one wife already."

"She mysteriously disappeared," replied Esther. "Some day you will find her skeleton, poor thing!"

"Do you think so?" said Catherine gravely. "How fascinating he is! He makes me shiver!"

When Catherine begged to have every thing begun again, Wharton hesitated. Esther's work was not to his taste, but he was not at all sure that she would do equally well if she tried to imitate his own manner.

"You know I wanted Miss Dudley to put more religious feeling and force into her painting," said he, "but you all united and rode me down."

"I will look like a real angel this time," said Catherine. "Now I know what it is you want."

"I am more than half on her side," went on Wharton. "I am not sure that she is wrong. It all comes to this: is religion a struggle or a joy? To me it is a terrible battle, to be won or lost. I like your green dress with the violets. Whose idea was that?"

"Petrarch's. You know I am Laura. St. Cecilia has the dress which Laura wore in church when Petrarch first saw her."

"No!" said Wharton, after another pause, and long study of the two figures. "Decidedly I will not rub you out; but I mean to touch up Petrarch."

"O! You won't spoil the likeness!"

"Not at all! But if I am going to posterity by your side I want some expression in my face. Petrarch was a man of troubles."

"You promise not to change the idea?"

"I promise to look at you as long as you look at me," said Wharton gloomily.

Meanwhile Esther had a talk with Mr. Hazard which left her more in doubt than ever as to what she had best do. He urged her to begin something new and to do it in a more strenuous spirit.

"You are learning from Wharton," said he. "Why should you stop at the very moment when you have most to gain?"

"I am learning nothing but what I knew before," she answered sadly. "He can teach only grand art and I am fit only for trifles."

"Try one more figure!"

Esther shook her head.

"My Cecilia is a failure," she went on. "Mr. Wharton said it would be, and he was right. I should do no better next time, unless I took his design and carried it out exactly as he orders."

"One's first attempt is always an experiment. Try once more!"

"I should only spoil your church. In the middle of your best sermon your audience would see you look up here and laugh."

"You are challenging compliments."

"What I could do nicely would be to paint squirrels and monkeys playing on vines round the choir, or daisies and buttercups in a row, with one tall daisy in each group of five. That is the way for a woman to make herself useful."

"Be serious!"

"I feel more solemn than Mr. Wharton's great figure of John of Patmos. I am going home to burn my brushes and break my palette. What is the use of trying to go forward when one feels iron bars across one's face?"

"Be reasonable, Miss Dudley! If Wharton is willing to teach, why not be willing to learn? You are not to be the judge. If I think your work good, have I not a right to call on you for it?"

"Oh, yes! You have a right to call, and I have a right to refuse. I will paint no more religious subjects. I have not enough soul. My St. Cecilia looks like a nursery governess playing a waltz for white-cravated saints to dance by." There was a tone of real mortification in Esther's voice as she looked once more at the figure on the wall, and felt how weak it seemed by the side of Wharton's masculine work. Then she suddenly changed her mind and did just what he asked: "If Mr. Wharton will consent, I will begin again, and paint it all over."

A woman could easily have seen that she was torn in opposite directions by motives of a very contrary kind, but Mr. Hazard did not speculate on this subject; he was glad to carry his point, and let the matter rest there. It was agreed that the next morning Wharton should decide upon the proper course to be taken, and if he chose to reject her figure, she should begin it again. Esther and Catherine went home, but Esther was ill at ease. That her St. Cecilia did not come up to the level of her ambition was a matter of course, and she was prepared for the disappointment. Whose first attempt in a new style ever paired with its conception? She felt that Mr. Hazard would think her wayward and weak. She could not tell him the real reason of her perplexity. She would have liked to work on patiently under Wharton's orders without a thought of herself, but how could she do so when Hazard was day by day coming nearer and nearer until already their hands almost touched. If she had not liked him, the question could easily have been settled, but she did like him, and when she said this to herself she turned scarlet at the thought that he liked her, and--what should she do?

With a heavy heart she made up her mind that there was but one thing to be done; she must retreat into her own house and bar the doors. If he did not see that such an intimacy was sure to make trouble for him, she, who felt, if she did not see, the gulf that separated them, must teach him better.

Whether she would have held to this wise and prudent course against his entreaties and Wharton's commands will never be known, for the question, which at the moment seemed to her so hard to decide, was already answered by fates which left her no voice in the matter. The next morning when the two girls, rather later than usual, reached the south door of the church where a stern guardian always stood to watch lest wolves entered under pretense of business, they saw a woman standing on the steps and gazing at them as they approached from the avenue. In this they found nothing to surprise them, but as they came face to face with her they noticed that the stranger's dress and features were peculiar and uncommon even in New York, the sink of races. Although the weather was not cold, she wore a fur cap, picturesque but much worn, far from neat, and matching in dirt as in style a sort of Polish or Hungarian capote thrown over her shoulders. Her features were strong, coarse and bloated; her eyes alone were fine. When she suddenly spoke to Esther her voice was rough, like her features; and though Esther had seen too little of life to know what depths of degradation such a face and voice meant, she drew back with some alarm. The woman spoke in French only to ask whether this was the church of St. John. Replying shortly that it was, Esther passed in without waiting for another question; but as she climbed the narrow and rough staircase to her gallery, she said to Catherine who was close behind:

"Somewhere I have seen that woman's eyes."

"So have I!" answered Catherine, in a tone of suppressed excitement so unusual that Esther stopped short on the step and turned round.

"Don't you know where?" asked Catherine without waiting to be questioned.

"Where was it?"

"In my picture! Mr. Wharton gave me her eyes. I am sure that woman is his wife."

"Catherine, you shall go back to Colorado. You have been reading too many novels. You are as romantic as a man."

Catherine did not care whether she were romantic or not; she knew the woman was Wharton's wife.

"Perhaps she means to kill him," she ran on in a blood-curdling tone. "Wouldn't it be like Mr. Wharton to be stabbed to the heart on the steps of a church, just as his great work was done? Do you know I think he would like it. He is dying to be tragic like the Venetians, and have some one write a poem about him." Then after a moment's pause, she added, in the same indifferent tone of voice: "All the same, if he's not there, I mean to go back and look out for him. I'm not going to let that woman kill him if I can help it!"

A warm dispute arose between the two girls which continued after they reached their scaffold and found that Wharton was not there. Esther declared that Catherine should not go back; it was ridiculous and improper; Mr. Wharton would laugh in her face and think her bold and impertinent; the woman was probably a beggar who wanted to see Mr. Hazard; and when all this was of no avail Esther insisted that Catherine should not go alone. Catherine, on her part, declared that she was not afraid of the woman, or of any woman, or man either, or of Mr. Wharton, and that she meant to walk down the avenue and meet him, and tell him that this person was there. She was on the point of doing what she threatened when they saw Wharton himself cross the church beneath and slowly climb the stairs.

The two girls, dismissing their alarm as easily as they had taken it up, turned to their own affairs again. In a few minutes Wharton appeared on the scaffolding and went to his regular work-place. After a time they saw him coming to their corner.

He looked paler than usual and more abstracted, and, what was unusual, he carried a brush in his hand, as though he had broken off his work without thinking what he was doing. He hardly noticed them, but sat down, holding the brush with both hands, though it was wet. For some time he looked at the Cecilia without a word; then he began abruptly:

"You're quite right! It's not good! It's not handled in a large way or in keeping with the work round it. You might do it again much better. But it is you and it is she! I would leave it. I will leave it! If necessary I could in a few days paint it all over and make it harmonize, but I should spoil it. I can draw better and paint better, but I can't make a young girl from Colorado as pure and fresh as that. To me religion is passion. To reach Heaven, you must go through hell, and carry its marks on your face and figure. I can't paint innocence without suggesting sin, but you can, and the church likes it. Put your own sanctity on the wall beside my martyrdom!"

Esther thought it would be civil on her part to say something at this point, but Wharton's remarks seemed to be made to no one in particular, and she was not quite certain that they were meant for her in spite of the words. He did not look at her. She was used to his peculiar moods and soliloquies, and had learned to be silent at such times. She sat silent now, but Catherine, who took greater liberties with him, was bolder.

"Why can't you paint innocence?" she asked.

"I am going to tell you," he replied, with more quickness of manner. "It is to be the subject of my last lecture. Ladies, school must close to-day."

Esther and Catherine glanced at each other. "You are going to send us away?" asked Catherine in a tone of surprise.

"You must go for the present," answered Wharton. "I mean to tell you the reason, and then you will see why I can't paint innocence as you can. As a lecture on art, my life is worth hearing, but don't interrupt the story or you will lose it. Begin by keeping in your mind that twenty years ago I was a ragged boy in the streets of Cincinnati. The drawing master in a public school to which I went, said I had a natural talent for drawing, and taught me all he knew. Then a little purse was made up for me and I was sent to Paris. Not yet twenty years old, I found myself dropped into that great sewer of a city, a shy, ill-clothed, ill-fed, ill-educated boy, knowing no more of the world above me than a fish knows of the birds. For two years

I knocked about in a studio till my money was used up, and then I knew enough to be able to earn a few francs to keep me alive. Then I went down to Italy and of course got a fever. I came back at last to Paris, half-fed, dyspeptic and morbid. I had visions, and the worst vision of my life I am going to tell you.

"It was after I had been some years at work and had got already a little reputation among Americans, that I was at my worst. Nothing seemed real. What earned me my first success was an attempt I made to paint the strange figures and fancies which possessed me. I studied nothing but the most extravagant subjects. For a time nothing would satisfy me but to draw from models at moments of intense suffering and at the instant of death. Models of that kind do not offer themselves and are not to be bought. I made friends with the surgeons and got myself admitted to one of the great hospitals. I happened to be there one day when a woman was brought in suffering from an overdose of arsenic. This was the kind of subject I wanted. She was fierce, splendid, a priestess of the oracle! Tortured by agony and clinging to it as though it were a delight! The next day I came back to look for her: she was then exhausted and half dead. She was a superb model, and I took an interest in her. When she grew better I talked with her and found that she was a sort of Parisian Pole with a strange history. She had been living as an actress at one of the small theaters, and had attempted suicide in sheer disgust with life. I had played with the same idea for years. We had both struggled with the world and hated it. Her imagination was more morbid than my own, and in her quieter moments, when her affections were roused, she was wonderfully tender and devoted. When she left the hospital she put herself under my protection. I believe she loved me, and no one had ever loved me before. I know she took possession of me, body and soul. I married her. I would just as willingly have jumped into the Seine with her if she had preferred it. For three months we lived together while I finished the picture which I called the Priestess of Delphi, painted from my drawings of her in her agony. The picture made a great noise in Paris, and brought me some new friends, among the rest one who, I think, really saved me from Charenton. Hazard called at my studio just as my troubles were beginning to tear me to pieces. My wife had the temper of a fury, and all the vices of Paris. Excitement was her passion; she could not stand the quiet of an artist's life; yet her Bohemian instincts came over her only in waves, and when they left her in peace she still had splendid qualities that held me to her. Hazard came in upon us one day in the middle of a terrible scene when she was threatening again to take her own life, and trying, or pretending to try to take mine. When he came in, she disappeared. The next I heard of her, she was back on the stage--lost! I was worn out; my nervous system was all gone. Then Hazard came to my help and took me off with him to the south of Europe. Our first stage was to Avignon and Vaucluse, and there I found how curiously my experience had affected my art. I had learned to adore purity and repose, but I could never get hold of my ideal. Fifty times I tried to draw Laura as I wanted to realize her and every time I failed. I knew the secret of Petrarch and I could not tell it. My wife came between me and my thought. All life took form in my hands as a passion. If I could learn again to paint a child, or any thing that had not the world in its eyes, I should be at peace at last."

As he paused here, and seemed again to be musing over St. Cecilia, Esther's curiosity made her put in a word,

"And your wife?"--she asked.

"My wife?" he repeated in his abstracted tone, "I never saw her again till this morning when I met her on the steps of the church."

"Then it was your wife?" cried Catherine.

"You saw her?" he asked with a touch of bitterness. "I won't ask what you thought of her."

"I knew her by her eyes," cried Catherine. "I thought she meant to shoot you, and when you came in I was just going to warn you. Now you see, Esther, I was right."

Wharton leaned over and took Catherine's hand. "Thank you," said he. "I believe you are my good angel. But you remind me of what I came to say. The woman is quite capable of that or of any other scandal, and of course Hazard's church must not be exposed to such a risk. I shall come here no longer for the present, neither must you. I am bound to take care of my friends."

"But you!" said Esther. "What are you going to do?"

"I? Nothing! What can I do?"

"Do you mean," said Catherine, with a comical fierceness in her voice as though she wanted herself to take the French actress in hand, "do you mean to let that woman worry you how she likes?"

"The fault was mine," replied Wharton. "I gave her my life. After all she is my wife and I can't help it. I have promised to meet her this afternoon at my studio."

Even to these two girls there was something so helpless in Wharton's ideas of life that they protested against his conduct. Catherine was speechless with inability to understand what he meant. Esther boldly interfered.

"You must do nothing without advice," said she. "Wait till Mr. Hazard comes and consult him. If you can't see him, promise me to go to my uncle, Mr. Murray, and let him take charge of this woman. You will ruin your whole life if you let her into it again."

"It is ruined already," answered Wharton gloomily. "I had that one chance of happiness and I can never have another."

Nevertheless he promised to wait for Hazard, and the two girls obediently bade him good-by. Catherine's eyes were full of tears as he held her hand and begged her pardon for his rudeness. A little romance was passing out of her life. She went down the stairs after Esther without a word. As they left the church they saw the woman on the pavement outside, still walking up and down; Catherine passed her with a glance of repulsion and defiance that made the woman turn and watch her till they disappeared down the avenue.

An hour afterwards a quick step hurried up the stair, and Hazard, evidently much disturbed, appeared on the scaffolding. He found Wharton where the two girls had left him, sitting alone before St. Cecilia, the broken brush still in his hands, and his left hand red with the wet paint. His face was paler than ever, and over the left temple was a large red spot, as though he had been pressing his hands to his forehead. Hazard looked for a moment at the white face, contrasting painfully with its ghastly spot of intense red, and then spoke with assumed indifference: "So she has turned up again!" Wharton returned his look with a weak smile which made his face still more horrible, and slowly answered:

"I have worse news than that!"

"More bad news!" said Hazard.

"Tell me what you think," continued Wharton in the same dreamy tone. "You see that Cecilia there?"

Hazard glanced at the figure and back to Wharton without speaking. Presently Wharton added with a smile of inexpressible content:

"Well! I love her."

Chapter VI

ESTHER'S regrets on quitting her work at the church lasted not so long as Catherine's, though they were more serious. She had already begun to feel alarmed about her father's condition, and nothing but his positive order had induced her to leave him even for a few hours every day. She had seen that his strength steadily failed; he suffered paroxysms of pain; he lost consciousness more than once; and although he insisted to the last on acting as though he were well, his weakness increased until he could no longer sit out a game of whist, but was forced to lie on the sofa in his library where he liked to see every visitor who came to the house. He required that every thing about him should go on as usual, and not only made Esther go regularly to her work, but took keen interest in hearing from her and Catherine all that was said and done at the church. He delighted in laughing at Catherine about her romantic relations with Wharton, but he made no jokes about Mr. Hazard. He thought from the first that this intimacy might be a serious matter for Esther, but he would not again interfere in her affairs, and feared making things worse by noticing them. He watched Hazard sharply, until Esther had the uncomfortable sense of feeling that her father's eyes were never far away from the clergyman when he came to the house. She knew, or fancied she knew, every thought in her father's mind, and his silence embarrassed her more than criticism could have done. She asked herself in vain why her father, disliking the clergy as she knew he did, should suddenly admit a clergyman into his intimacy. In truth, Mr. Dudley looked on himself as no longer having a right to speak; his feelings and prejudices were to be kept out of her life; but he could watch, and the longer he watched, the more intense his interest became.

When Esther and Catherine returned from the church with their account of Wharton's wife, their first act was to tell the story to Mr. Dudley, who lay on his sofa and listened with keen interest.

"I suppose you meant to come back for my revolver," said he to Catherine, whose little explosions of courage always amused him. "I think I could almost have crawled round to see you take a shot at your French friend as she started for you."

"Oh, no!" said Catherine modestly. "I would have given the revolver to Mr. Wharton."

"Don't do it, Catherine! Wharton could not hit the church door with it. Suppose he had shot you instead of the other woman!"

"Of course!" said Catherine reflectively. "He wouldn't know how to use a revolver, would he? I suppose I ought to teach him."

"Better not!" said Mr. Dudley. "Keep him under. You may have to talk with him one of these days, after you have settled your little misunderstanding with his wife."

Catherine took chaff with such gravity that even Mr. Dudley could not always make out whether she was in jest or earnest. She had a quaint, serious way of accepting any sort of challenge and going it better, as Strong expressed it, which left her assailants wholly in the dark. Mr. Dudley wanted to stop any romantic nonsense between her and Wharton, but could never quite make out whether she cared for him or not. Esther thought not.

That evening they all hoped that Hazard would come in to tell them what other scenes had occurred, and, under this little excitement, Mr. Dudley felt strong enough to appear like himself, although he dared not rise from his sofa. At about eight o'clock they were gratified. Mr. Hazard appeared, and was received with such cordiality and intimacy as went far to make him feel himself a member of the family.

"Thank you," said Mr. Dudley. "We have done nothing but run to the watchtower to see if you were coming. Tell us quickly the ghastly news. We are prepared for the worst."

"If you read Turgenieff," replied Hazard, "you can imagine the kind of experience we have had. I feel as though I had stolen a chapter from one of his stories."

"No matter! Spoil it promptly! We never read any thing."

"May I have first a cup of tea, Miss Dudley? Thank you! That woman has left a taste on my palate that all the tea in China will never wash off. Where shall I begin?"

"Where we left off," said Esther. "We left Mr. Wharton in the church at eleven o'clock, and the woman marching up and down outside."

"At noon I found her there, and knew her at once, though it is ten years since I last saw her. She is a person whom one does not forget. I asked her what she wanted. It seemed that Wharton, in his confusion, had told her to come to his studio without saying where it was; and she was waiting for him to come out again. I gave her the address and sent her away. Then I went up to Wharton whom I found in a strange state of mind; he seemed dazed and showed no interest in the affair. He would not talk of his wife at all until I forced him. At length, after a struggle, as he said that Miss Dudley had told him to go to her uncle, Mr. Murray, I got him into a carriage and we drove to Mr. Murray's office. The upshot was that Mr. Murray and I took the matter into our hands and decided to meet the woman ourselves in his company. At the hour fixed, we went, all three of us, to the studio.

"It needed at least three of us to deal with that one woman. When I saw her in Paris she was still young and handsome, with superb eyes and a kind of eastern tread. You could imagine her, when she did not speak, as Semiramis, Medea, Clytemnestra! Except that when you saw a little more of her, you felt that she was only a heroine of a cheap theater. Wharton could not have been fascinated by her, if, at that time of his life, he had ever known a refined woman or mixed at all in the world; but she certainly had a gypsy charm, and seemed to carry oceans of Sahara and caravans of camels about with her. When she was in one of her furies, it was an echo of the whole Greek drama. This, you must recollect, was ten years ago, and even then she was spoiled by being coarse and melodramatic, but now she is a horror. She suggests nothing but the penitentiary. When she saw that there were three of us, she flew into a whirlwind of passion, and screamed French that I was glad to find I could not wholly understand. Her dialect must come from the worst class of Parisian thieves. I should have been glad to understand less than I did. Every now and then she interrupted this Billingsgate, and seemed to think that her dignity required a loftier style, and she poured out on us whole pages of cheap melodrama. She began by flinging her fur cap and cloak on the floor and striking a stage attitude. She wanted to know who we were; by what right did we mix ourselves in this affair and come between a villain and his victim! Then she turned on Wharton and began gesticulating and throwing herself into contortions like a Maenad, repeating again and again that he was her husband, an 'infame,' a 'lache,' and that she would take his life if she were not given her rights. She drew herself up in all her height, and growled in her deepest voice: 'Je vais t'ecr-r-r-raser!' Then she changed her tone and sobbed violently that on second thoughts she preferred to kill herself, and finally tore a small stage dagger from her breast and proposed to kill us all and herself too."

"How many did she manage in the end?" asked Mr. Dudley.

"How did Mr. Wharton bear it?" asked Esther.

"Wharton stood it very well," replied Hazard. "He was sitting near her, and now and then she made a rush at him as though she really meant to strike him. He never moved, or spoke, or took his eyes away from her. I think he was overcome by association; he thought himself back in Paris ten years ago."

"Doubtless this excellent woman has faults, owing to a defective education," said Mr. Dudley with his usual dry, half-smile. "We must make allowances for them. I am more curious to know whether she got the better of my astute brother-in-law."

"Mr. Murray took an unfair advantage over her," said Hazard. "He had taken the precaution to post a police officer in the next room, and after the woman had exhausted herself, and I think too had worn off the effects of the brandy she reeked with, he told her that she would go instantly to the police station if she did not behave herself. I think her imagination must have taught her that an American police station might be something very terrible, for in a few minutes she quieted down and was only eager for money."

"I suppose Murray means to terrify this poor creature into a sacrifice of her rights?" said Mr. Dudley.

"Wharton will have to settle an annuity on her, in order to get her back to Europe and keep her there. In return, she has got to consent to a divorce. Mr. Murray insists on this as his first condition. Wharton began to say that she was his wife, and that he was bound to take care of her, until at last Mr. Murray told him to take himself off or he would have no more to do with the case. So the woman, on receiving some money on the spot, consents to deal with Mr. Murray directly, on his terms, and Wharton leaves town till the papers are drawn up and the woman packed off.

He has had a shock which will prevent his working for some time."

"He may not feel like painting saints," said Mr. Dudley, "but I should think he was in good form for painting sinners. Is there no room for a Jezebel in your portrait gallery?"

Mr. Dudley was too weak for late hours and Hazard went away early. As he went he said he would come again to tell them the next chapter, if there was one.

"Be quick about it!" said Mr. Dudley. "I am like the Sultan who cut off his wives' heads because they would not tell him stories fast enough. It is not convenient for me to wait."

To Esther this evening was the last when the stars shone bright and clear. The next morning her glimpse of blue sky had vanished and the rigor of the storm began.

She was waked by the news that in the night her father had been seized by another paroxysm, and that although better, he was excessively weak. He had forbidden his attendants to call her, on the cool calculation that he should probably pull through this attack, and that she would need all her strength for the next. When Esther came down to his room, she found him in a state of complete prostration, so that his doctors had forbidden him to speak or even to listen. They no longer talked with him, but gave their orders to her, and she took charge of the sick-room at once with all its responsibilities and fatigues. After a consultation of very few moments, the physicians told her plainly that there was no hope; her father might linger a short time, but any sudden emotion would kill him on the spot.

During the day he rallied a little and in the evening was stronger. Esther, who had been all day in his room, rested till midnight and then took her regular watch by his side. She knew that there was no hope and that her father himself was only anxious for the end, yet to see him suffer and slowly fade out was terrible. At such moments, tears are forbidden. Esther had been told that she must not give way to agitation, under the risk of killing her father, who lay dozing, half-conscious, with his face turned towards her. Whenever his eyes opened they rested on hers. In the dim light she watched his motions, and it seemed to her that he was also watching hers. She wondered whether he could feel stronger because she was near him. Was he afraid? He, who had never to her knowledge shrunk from any danger, and who in the army had shown reckless indifference even when he supposed his wounds to be mortal, was now watching her as though he feared to have her leave his side. In his extreme weakness, unable to lift his head, his mind evidently beginning to wander, perhaps he felt the need of her companionship, and dreaded solitude and death as she did. For half the night she pondered over this weakening of the will in the face of omnipotence crushing out the last spark of life, and was doubly startled when, the nurse coming to relieve her at six o'clock, she leaned over to kiss her father's forehead and found him looking at her in his old humorous way, while, in a low whisper, speaking slowly, as though he would not yield to the enemy that clutched his heart, he said:

"It's not so bad, Esther, when you come to it."

The tears started into Esther's eyes. It was only with an effort more violent than she had thought was in her power, that she forced herself to smile. Now that she had come to it, she thought it was very bad; worse than any thing she had ever imagined; she wanted to escape, to run away, to get out of life itself, rather than suffer such pain, such terror, such misery of helplessness; but after an instant's pause, her father whispered again, though his voice died away in weakness:

"Laugh, Esther, when you're in trouble! Say something droll! then you're safe. I saw the whole regiment laugh under fire at Gettysburg."

This was more than she could bear, and she had to hurry out of the room. She had fancied him yielding to fear and finding courage in her companionship. Suddenly she became aware that, with death's hand on his throat and a brain reeling in exhaustion, he was trying to teach her how to meet what life had to bring. The lesson was one she could not easily forget.

So she went to her bed, in the cold, gray dawn of a winter's day, with the tears still running down her face. When she woke again the day was already waning, a dripping, wasting thaw, when smoking and soot-defiled snow added sadness to the sad sky. Esther, on opening her eyes, saw Catherine sitting quietly before the fire, reading, or pretending to read. She was keeping guard lest Esther should be disturbed.

"He is no worse," she said, when Esther raised her head. "I was at his door five minutes ago. Mrs. Murray is there and so is the doctor. You are not wanted and they sent word that you were not to be disturbed."

Esther was glad to lie still a few minutes and collect her strength. It was pleasant to look at Catherine, the healthiest and most cheery of girls, after having under one's eyes a long night of terror.

"Professor Strong has been here this morning and I saw him," ran on Catherine. "He sent for me because he would not have you disturbed. He got back from St. Louis last night, and will come round here again this afternoon. Mr. Hazard has been here, too, and says he shall stop again in the evening."

This report required no answer. Esther felt the stronger for knowing that her friends were at her side, and that she could count on their help. Catherine ran on in the same vein.

"Mr. Hazard says that Mr. Wharton has left town and will not return until Mr. Murray sends for him. I think he might have left some message for me, to ask me to be true to him or something, but Mr. Hazard says he just went off to Boston without a word to any body. I have more than half a mind to desert him and go back to Colorado."

"If you leave me now, Catherine--"

"Oh! I don't mean to leave you, but I must earn my living. Let me take my watch with your father to-night! You will think you have struck a professional."

Esther refused, but Catherine did rather more than her share of work notwithstanding, and more than once Mr. Dudley, opening his eyes, found her at the head of his bed and greeted her with a faint smile.

He passed the day without much sign of change. Esther was repeatedly called from his side to see persons whom she could not send away. Her aunt was with her till night. Strong came in and sat with her while she tried to dine. So long as daylight lasted she felt no sense of loneliness or desertion, and her courage remained fairly steady; but when she had sent home her aunt and cousin in order to begin her watch earlier than the previous night, her fears returned, her heart sank, and she begged Catherine to stay with her. The two girls began their watch together. Mr. Dudley seemed pleased to have them with him.

Presently a nurse came with a message that Mr. Hazard was below, and had asked to see Esther for a moment. Mr. Dudley overheard the message, and whispered to his daughter:

"Tell him I am sorry not to see him! Say I am just going out!"

He spoke dreamily, as though half asleep, and Esther, as she leaned over him, trying to catch his words, doubted whether he was quite conscious. He muttered a few more words: "I won't interfere, but the church--." She caught no more, and he dozed off again into silence. After watching him a few moments, Esther beckoned to Catherine to take her chair, and slipped out of the room. She wanted to see Hazard, for, strange as it seemed to her, he had become her most intimate friend, and she could not send him away at such a moment.

She found him at the foot of the stairs, and there they remained standing for a few moments, talking in low tones, by the light of a dim gas-burner.

"I want to help you," he said. "I am used to such scenes and you are not. You need help though you may not ask for it."

She shook her head: "I am a miserable coward," she said; "but we are beyond help now, and I must learn endurance."

"You will over-tax your strength," he urged. "Remember, there is no excitement so great as to stand for the first time in face of eternity, as you are doing."

"I suppose it must be so," she answered. "Every thing seems unreal. I can't even realize my father's illness. Your voice sounds far-off, as though you were calling to me out of the distance and darkness. I hardly know what we are saying, or why we are here. I never felt so before."

"It is over-excitement and fatigue," he replied soothingly. "Do you feel afraid, too?"

"Terribly!" she answered; "I want to run away. But I think death excites almost more than it frightens. My father laughs at it even now."

"I am more concerned about you," continued Hazard. "I can do nothing for him, and you may feel sure that for him all the worst is over. Will you let me stay here on the chance of your needing help?"

"I have already sent away my aunt and George Strong," she said. "Do not feel alarmed about me. Women have more strength than men."

As he left the house, he thought to himself that this woman at least had more strength than most men. He could not forget her pale face, or her dreamy voice and far-off eyes as she had told him her feelings. Most women would have asked him for religious help and consolation. She had gently put his offers aside. She seemed to him like a wandering soul, lost in infinite space, but still floating on, with her quiet air of confidence as though she were a part of nature itself, and felt that all nature moved with her.

"I almost think," said Hazard to himself, "that she could give a lesson in strength to me. It seems rather unnecessary, my offering to give one to her."

Yet Esther felt little like giving strength to any one. As she returned to the sick-room and slipped back into the chair which Catherine quitted, the image of Hazard faded from her mind, and the idea that he could help her, except by his sympathy and friendship, never entered it. After a time her father opened his eyes again and looked at her. She bent over him, and he whispered: "Give me your hand!" She took his hand, and for some time he lay with his eyes open, as though watching her. She could only wonder what was in his mind; perhaps disconnected dreams with intervals of partial consciousness, as now, followed by more vague visions and hurrying phantasms; but she imagined that he had meant not so much to ask for the strength of her hand as to give her die will and courage of his own, and she felt only the wish that he might not doubt her answer to the call. Although he soon dozed again, she did not alter her position, but sat hour after hour, only making way for the nurse who came to give him stimulants which had less and less effect. Her watch ended at two o'clock, when she sent Catherine to bed, but remained herself until the gray dawn had passed and the sun was high in the heavens. She meant her father to know, as long as he knew any thing, that her hand was in his. Not until the doctor assured her that he was no longer conscious, did her long walk into the shadow of death at last end. When Mrs. Murray came, she found Esther still there, her face paler than ever, with dark rings round her eyes, and looking worn and old. As she spoke, her eyes constantly filled with tears, and her nerves were strung up to a tension which made her aunt promptly intervene and insist on her taking rest. Esther obeyed like a worn-out child.

So died William Dudley, and was buried under the ice and snow of winter, while his daughter went on alone to meet the buffets of life. It was in the first days of February that Esther looked about her and seemed to feel that the world had changed. She said to herself that youth was gone. What was she to do with middle-life? At twenty-six to be alone, with no one to interpose as much as a shadow across her path, was a strange sensation; it made her dizzy, as though she were a solitary bird flying through mid-air, and as she looked ahead on her aerial path, could see no tie more human than that which bound her to Andromeda and Orion.

To this moral strain was added the reaction from physical fatigue. For a week or two after her father's death, Esther felt languid, weary and listless. She could not sleep. A voice, a bar of music, the sight of any thing unusual, affected her deeply. She could not get back to her regular interests. First came the funeral with its inevitable depression and fatigue; then came days of vacancy, with no appetite for work and no chance for amusement. She took refuge in trifles, but the needle and scissors are terrible weapons for cutting out and trimming not so much women's dresses as their thoughts. She had never been a reader, and perhaps for that reason her mind had all the more run into regions of fancy and imagination. She caught half an idea in the air, and tossed it for amusement. In these days of unrest she tossed her ideas more rapidly than ever. Most women are more or less mystical by nature, and Esther had a vein of mysticism running through a practical mind.

The only person outside her family whom she saw was Hazard. He was either at the house or in some way near her almost every day. He took charge of the funeral services, and came to make inquiries, to bring messages, or to suggest an occupation, until he was looked upon as one of the household. Once or twice, the week after the funeral, he came in the evening, and asked for a cup of tea. Then Catherine sat by and dozed while Esther talked mysticism with Hazard, who was himself a mystic of the purest water. By this time Esther had learned to look on the physical life, the daily repetition of breakfast and dinner, as the unreal part of existence, and apologized to herself for conceding so much to habit, or put it down to Catherine's account. Her illusions were not serious; perhaps she had for this short instant a flash of truth, and by the light of her father's deathbed, saw life as it is; but, while the mood lasted, nothing seemed real except the imagination, and nothing true but the spiritual. In this atmosphere Hazard was always happy, for he reveled in the voluptuousness of poetry, and found peace in the soul of a dandelion; but to share his subtlest fancies with a woman who could understand and feel them, was to reach a height of poetry that trembled on the verge of realizing heaven. His great eyes shone with the radiance of paradise, and his delicate thin features expressed beatitude, as he discussed with Esther the purity of the soul, the victory of spirit over matter, and the peace of infinite love.

Of her regular occupations Esther kept up only such as were duties, but among them she was true to her little hospital, and went once or twice a week to see the children who clamored for her visits. She went alone, for she liked solitude, and was glad to give Catherine an excuse for escaping to gayer houses and seeing brighter society. About a fortnight after her father's death, one Saturday afternoon when she felt more solitary than ever, and more restless because her long quiet had begun to bring back her strength, she went to the hospital where the children welcomed her with delight. She took her old seat and looked through the yellow eyes of the fire-dogs for inspiration; opened a package and distributed small presents, little Japanese umbrellas, fans, doll's shoes and such small change of popularity; and, at last, obeying the cries for more story, she went on with the history of Princess Lovely in her Cocoanut Island, besieged by whales and defended by talking elephants and monkeys. She had hardly begun when the door opened and again Mr. Hazard entered. This time Esther blushed.

Hazard sat down, and finding that she soon tired of story-telling, he took it up, and gave a chapter of his own which had wild success, so that the children begged for more and more, until five o'clock was past and twilight coming on. As Esther was on foot, Mr. Hazard said he would see her to her door, and they walked away together.

"Do you know that Wharton has come back?" said he as they reached the street. "His affair is settled; the woman sailed yesterday for Europe, and he is to have a divorce. Your uncle has managed it very well."

"Will Mr. Wharton go to work again at the church?" asked Esther.

"He begins at once. He asked me to find out for him whether you would begin with him."

"Did he say whether he wanted me or Catherine?" asked Esther with a laugh.

Hazard laughed in reply. "I think myself he would be satisfied to get Miss Brooke, but you must not underrate your own merits. He wants you both."

"I am afraid he must give us up," said Esther, with a little sigh. "Certainly I can't come, and if he wants Catherine, he will have to come himself and get her; but he will find Catherine not easy to get."

They discussed Wharton and his affairs till they reached Esther's house, and she said: "It is not yet six o'clock. I can give you a cup of tea if you will come in?"

She could not do less than offer him this small hospitality, and yet--Catherine was not at home. They went up to the library, and Esther ordered tea to be brought.

She took off her bonnet and cloak, and threw them on a chair. She sat down before the fire, and he stood on the hearth-rug looking at her while she made tea in the twilight. At this moment he was more hopelessly in love than any other Church of England clergyman within the diocese of New York.

"What are then your plans for the future?" he asked, after they had chatted for some time on the subject of Esther's painting. "If you will not return to help us, what do you look forward to doing?"

"I want to take Catherine and go abroad," answered Esther. "If I can get my uncle and aunt to go, we shall start in the spring."

At this announcement Hazard seemed to receive a shock. He turned suddenly to her, his eyes sparkling with passion: "Take me with you! What shall I do without you!" He seized her hand and poured out a torrent of broken protests: "I love you with all my heart and soul! Don't leave me alone in this horrible city! I shall die of disgust if you desert me! You are the only woman I ever loved! Ah! You must love me!"

Esther, trembling, bewildered, carried away by this sudden and violent attack, made at first a feeble effort to withdraw her hand and to gasp a protest, but the traitor within her own breast was worse than the enemy without. For the moment all her wise resolutions were swept away in a wave of tenderness; she seemed to come suddenly on a summer sea, sparkling with hope and sunshine, the dreary sand-banks of her old life vanishing like a dream. She shut her eyes and found herself in his arms. Then in terror at what she had done, she tried again to draw back.

"No, no!" she said rapidly, trying to free herself. "You must not love me! You must let me go!"

"I love you! I adore you! I will never let you go!"

"You must! You do not know what you are doing! Ah! Let me go!"

"Tell me first that you love me!"

"No, no! I am not good enough for you. You must love some one who has her heart in your work."

"Tell me that you love me!" repeated Hazard.

"You do not know me! You must not love me! I shall ruin your life! I shall never satisfy you!"

Hazard caressed her only the more tenderly as he answered with the self-confidence which he put into all he did: "If my calling is so poor a thing that it cannot satisfy both our lives, I will have nothing more to do with it. I have more faith in us both. Promise to love me and I will take care of the rest."

"Ah!" gasped Esther, carried away by her own feelings and the vehemence of his love: "I am getting in deeper and deeper! What shall I do? Do not make me promise!"

"Then I will promise for both!" he said; and poor Esther ceased to struggle.

The same evening at dinner, Mrs. Murray remarked to her husband that she was becoming more and more uneasy about Esther's intimacy with Mr. Hazard.

"People are talking about it," she said. "It is really becoming a matter of public discussion."

"Do you suppose she would accept him?" asked Mr. Murray.

"How can I tell? She would say no, and then very likely do it. She is in the worst sort of a state of mind for an offer of that kind."

"Poor Dudley will rise from his grave," said Mr. Murray.

"He warned me to prevent such a match if I saw it coming," said Mrs. Murray; "but he did nothing to prevent it himself. He thought Esther was going to be very unhappy, and would make some such mistake. I would interfere, but it will only make matters worse. The thing has gone too far now."

"Take her away," said Mr. Murray.

"Where to? If you will go to Europe in the spring, we will take her over and leave her there with Catherine, but she may be married by that time."

"Give her a lecture," said Mr. Murray. "Show her that she is making a stupendous blunder!"

"Better show him!" said Mrs. Murray with a little resentment. "The blunder will be worse for him than for her."

"Explain it to her!" said he. "She has sense. Esther is a good girl, and I won't stand by and see her throw herself away on a church. I will speak to her myself if you don't."

"A nice piece of work you would make of it!" rejoined his wife. "No! If it is to be done, I suppose I must do it, but she will hate me all her life."

"Do it at once, then," said Mr. Murray. "The longer you put it off, the worse she will take it."

"I will talk with her to-morrow," replied Mrs. Murray; and the next day, when she went to take Esther to drive in the afternoon, her niece received her with an embarrassed air and a high color, and said:

"Aunt! I have something to tell you."

"Good heavens!" gasped Mrs. Murray.

"I am engaged to Mr. Hazard."

Chapter VII

THE instant Esther felt herself really loved, she met her fate as women will when the shock is once over. Hazard had wanted her to love him, had pursued and caught her. Now when she turned to him and answered his call, she seemed to take possession of him and lift him up. By the time he left her house this Saturday evening, he felt that he had found a soul stronger and warmer than his own, and was already a little afraid of it. Every man who has at last succeeded, after long effort, in calling up the divinity which lies hidden in a woman's heart, is startled to find that he must obey the God he summoned.

Esther herself was more astonished than Hazard at the force of this feeling which swept her away. She suddenly found herself passionately attached to a man, whom, down to the last moment, she had thought she could never marry, and now could no more imagine life without him than she could conceive of loving any one else. For the moment she thought that his profession was nothing to her; she could believe whatever he believed and do whatever he did; and if her love, backed by her will, were not strong enough to make his life her own, she cared little what became of her, and could look with indifference on life itself. So far as she was concerned she thought herself ready to worship Woden or Thor, if he did.

The next morning she could not let him preach without being near him, and she made Catherine go with her to St. John's. They took their seats, not in her own pew but in a corner, where no one should notice them under their veils. The experiment was full of peril, though Esther did not know it. This new excitement, coming so swiftly after a fortnight of exhaustion, threw her back into a state of extreme nervousness. Of course the scene of Saturday evening was followed by a sleepless night, and when Sunday morning came, her very restlessness made her hope that she should find repose and calm within the walls of the church. She went believing that she needed nothing so much as the quieting influence of the service, and she was not disappointed, for her sweetest associations were here, and as she glanced timidly up to the scaffolding where her romance had been acted, she felt at home and happy, in spite of the crowd of people who swarmed about her and separated her from the things she loved. In the background stood the solemn and awful associations of the last few weeks, the mysteries and terrors of death, drawing her from thought of earthly things to visions of another world. Full of these deep feelings, saturated with the elixir of love, Esther succumbed to the first notes of the church music. Tears of peaceful delight stood in her eyes. She glanced up towards her Cecilia on the distant wall, wondering at its childishness. How deep a meaning she could give it now, and how religious a feeling!

She was not conscious of rustling silks or waving feathers; she hardly saw the swarm of fashionable people about her; it seemed to her that her old life had vanished as though she were dead; her soul might have taken shelter in the body of some gray linnet for all that she thought or cared about the vanities of human society. She wanted only to be loved and to love, without being thought of, or noticed; to nestle in her own corner, and let the world go by.

Unluckily the world would not go by. This world which she wanted to keep at arms' length, was at church once for all, and meant to stay there; it felt itself at home, and she, with her exclusive griefs and joys, was the stranger. So long as the music lasted, all was sympathetic enough, but when Mr. Hazard read the service, he seemed far-off and strange. He belonged not to her but to the world; a thousand people had rights of property in him, soul and body, and called their claim religion. What had she to do with it? Parts of the service jarred on her ear. She began to take a bitter pleasure in thinking that she had nothing, not even religious ideas, in common with these people who came between her and her lover. Her fatigue steadily worked on her nerves. By the time the creed was read, she could not honestly feel that she believed a word of it, or could force herself to say that she ever should believe it.

With fading self-confidence she listened to the sermon. It was beautiful, simple, full of feeling and even of passion, but she felt that it was made for her, and she shrank before the thousand people who were thus let into the secret chambers of her heart. It treated of death and its mystery, covering ignorance with a veil of religious hope, and ending with an invocation of infinite love so intense in feeling and expression that, beautiful as it was, Esther forgot its beauties in the fear that the next word would reveal her to the world. This sort of publicity was new to her, and threw her back on herself until religion was forgotten in the alarm. She became more jealous than ever. What business had these strangers with her love? Why should she share it with them? When the service was over, she hurried Catherine away so quickly that they were both at home before the church was fairly empty.

This was the end of her short happiness. She knew that through the church door lay the only road to her duty and peace of mind. To see that the first happy impression had lasted barely half an hour, and instead of bringing peace, had brought irritation, was cause enough to alarm the most courageous young woman who ever rushed into the maelstrom of matrimony.

When they had reached home, she flung herself into a chair and covered her face with her hands.

"Catherine!" said she solemnly; "what am I to do? I don't like church."

"You would like your's amazingly," said Catherine, "if you had ever been to mine."

"Was your's worse?"

"If Mrs. Murray hadn't improved my manners so much, I should smile. Was mine worse? I wish you and Mr. Hazard would try it for a change. Mrs. Dyer would like to see you both undergoing discipline. Never joke about serious matters! You had better hold your tongue and be glad to live in a place where your friends let your soul alone."

"But I can't sit still and hear myself turned into a show! I can't share him with all Fifth Avenue. I want no one else to have him. To see him there devoting himself and me to a stupid crowd of people, who have as much right to him as I have, drives religion out of my head."

Catherine treated this weakness with high contempt.

"I might as well be jealous," said she, "of the people who look at Mr. Wharton's pictures, or read Petrarch's sonnets in my sweet translation. Did you ever hear that Laura found fault with Petrarch, or, if she did, that any one believed she was in earnest?"

"It is not the same thing," said Esther. "He believes in his church more than he does in me. If I can't believe in it, he will have to give me up."

"He, give you up!" said Catherine. "The poor saint! You know he is silly about you."

"He must give me up, if I am jealous of his congregation, and won't believe what he preaches," replied Esther mournfully.

"Why should you care what he preaches?" asked Catherine; "you never heard your aunt troubling her head about what Mr. Murray says when he goes to court."

"She is not forced to go to court with him," said Esther; "nor to be a mother to all the old women in the court-room; nor to say that she believes--believes--believes--when in her heart she doesn't believe a word."

Hazard appeared in the middle of this dispute, and Esther, troubled as she was, could not bear to distress him. She still meant to accept every thing and force herself to follow him in silence; she would go where he led, and never once raise her eyes to look for the horizon. As she said to herself quite seriously, though with a want of reverence that augured ill; "I will go down on my knees and help him, though he turn Bonze and burn incense to Buddha in my very studio!" His presence always soothed her. His gayety and affection never failed to revive her spirits and confidence.

"Wasn't it a good sermon?" said he to Catherine as he came in, with his boyish laugh of triumph. "Give me a little praise! I never got a word of encouragement from you in my life."

"I should as soon think of encouraging a whole herd of Texas cattle," answered Catherine. "What good can my praise do you?"

"You child of nature, don't you know that children of nature like you always grow wild and need no cultivation, but that we artificial flowers can't live without it?"

"I don't know how to cultivate," answered Catherine; "it is Esther you are thinking about."

Having announced this self-evident fact, Catherine walked off and left him to quiet Esther's alarms as he could. As she went she heard him turn to Esther and repeat his prayer that she should be gentle with him and give his sermon a word of praise.

"How can I stop to think whether it is good or not," said Esther, "when I hear you telling all our secrets to our whole visiting list? I could think of nothing but myself, and how I could get away."

"And whose secrets can I tell if not our own?" asked Hazard triumphant.

While he was with her Esther was peaceful and happy, but no sooner had he gone than her terrors began again.

"He will find me out, Catherine, and it will break my heart," she said. "I never knew I had a jealous temper. I am horribly narrow-minded. I'm not fit for him, and I knew it when he asked me. He will hate me when he finds what a wife he has got."

Catherine, who positively declined to recognize Mr. Hazard's superiority of mind over Esther, took this with unshaken fortitude. "If you can stand it, I guess he can," she remarked curtly. "Where do you expect the poor man to get a wife, if all of us say we are not fit for him?"

This view of the case amused Esther for a time, but not for long--the matter was too serious for any treatment but a joke, and joking made it more serious still. Try which way she would there was no escape from her anxiety. Hazard, who had foreseen some trouble from her old associations with loose religious opinion, had taken it for granted, with his usual self-confidence, that from the moment she came within the reach of his faith and took a place by his side she would find no difficulties that he could not easily overcome. "Love is the great magnet of life, and Religion," he said "is Love." Nothing could be simpler than his plan, as he explained to her. She had but to trust herself to him and all was sure to go well. So long as he was with her and could gently thrust aside every idea but that of their own happiness, all went as well as he promised; but unluckily for his plan, Esther had all her life been used to act for herself and to order others rather than take orders of any sort. The more confidently Hazard told her to leave every thing to him, the less it occurred to her to do so. She could no more allow him to come into her life and take charge of her thoughts than to go down into her kitchen and take charge of her cook. He might reason with her by the hour, and quite convince her that nothing was of the least consequence provided it were left entirely in his hands, but the moment he was out of sight she forgot that he was to be the keeper of her conscience, and, without a thought of her dependence, she resumed the charge of her own affairs.

Her first idea was to learn something of theology, in the hope of settling her foolish and ignorant doubts as to her fitness for her new position. No sooner did the thought occur to her than she set to work, like a young divinity student, to fit herself for her new calling. Her father's library contained a number of theological books, but these were of a kind that suited Mr. Dudley's way of thinking rather than that of the early fathers. As Esther knew nothing at all about the subject, except what she had gathered from listening to conversation, one book seemed to her as good as another, provided it dealt with the matter that interested her; but when Hazard came in and found her seated on a sofa, with a pile of these works about her, his hair rose on end, and he was forced gently to take them away under the promise of bringing her others of a more correct kind. These in their turn seemed to her not quite clear, and she asked for others still. He found himself, without warning, on the brink of a theological abyss. Unwilling to worry him; eager to accept whatever he told her he believed, but in despair at each failure to understand what it was, Esther became more and more uncomfortable and terrified.

"What would you do, Catherine, if you were in my place?" she asked.

"Let it alone!" said Catherine. "You didn't ask him to marry you. If he wants you, it's his business to suit himself to you."

"But I must go to his church," said Esther, "and sit at his communion."

"How many people at his church could tell you what they believe?" asked Catherine. "Your religion is just as good as theirs as long as you don't know what it is."

"One learns theology fast when one is engaged to be married," said Esther with a repentant face.

She was already sorry that she had tried to learn any thing about the subject, for she already knew too much, and yet a terrible fascination impelled her to read on about the nature of the trinity and the authority of tradition, until she lost patience with her own stupidity and burned to know what other people had to say on such matters. It occurred to her that she should like to have a quiet talk with George Strong.

Meanwhile Mrs. Murray, panic-stricken at learning the engagement, had sent at once for George. The messenger reached him on Sunday evening, a few hours after Esther told her aunt. Mystified by the urgent tone of Mrs. Murray's note, Strong came up at once, and found his uncle and aunt alone, after dinner, in their parlor, where Mr. Murray was quietly smoking a cigar, while his wife was holding a book in her hand and looking hard into the fire.

"George!" said his aunt solemnly; "do you know the mischief you and your friends have done?"

Strong stared. "You don't mean to tell me that Catherine has run off with Wharton?" said he. "She can't have done it, for I left Wharton not fifteen minutes ago at the club."

"No, not that! thank Heaven! Though if she hadn't more head than ever he had, that French wife of his might have given her more unhappiness than he is worth. No, it's not that! Catherine is the only sensible creature in the family."

Strong glared into the fire for a moment with a troubled air, and then looked at his aunt again. "No!" said he. "Esther hasn't joined the church. It can't be!"

"Yes!" said Mrs. Murray grimly.

"Caramba!" growled Strong, with a profusion of Spanish gutturals. Then after a moment's reflection, he added: "Poor child! Why should I care?"

"You irritate me more than your uncle does," broke out Mrs. Murray, at last losing patience. "Do you think I should be so distressed if Esther had only joined the church? I should like nothing better. What has happened is very different. She is engaged to Mr. Hazard."

Strong broke into a laugh, and Mr. Murray, with a quiet chuckle of humor, took his cigar out of his mouth to say:

"Let me explain this little matter to you, George! What troubles your aunt is not so much that Esther has joined the church as that she fears the church has joined Esther."

"The church has struck it rich this time;" remarked Strong without a sign of his first alarm. "Now we'll see what they'll make of her."

"The matter is too serious for joking;" said Mrs. Murray. "Either Esther will be unhappy for life, or Mr. Hazard will leave his church, or they will both be miserable whatever they do. I think you are bound to prevent it, since you are the one most to blame for getting them into it."

"I don't want to prevent it;" replied Strong. "It's a case of survival for the fittest. If Hazard can manage to convert Esther, let him do it. If not, let her take him in charge and convert him if she can. I'll not interfere."

"That is just the remark I had the honor to make to your aunt as you came in," said Mr. Murray. "Yesterday I wanted to stop it. To-day I want to leave it alone. They are both of them old enough to manage their own case. It has risen now to the dignity of a great cause, and I will be the devil's advocate."

"You are both of you intolerable," said Mrs. Murray, impatiently. "You talk about the happiness of Esther's life as though it were a game of poker. Tell me, George! what kind of a man is Mr. Hazard at heart?"

"Hazard is a priest at heart," replied Strong. "He has the qualities and faults of his class. I understand how this thing happened. He sees nothing good in the world that he does not instantly covet for the glory of God and the church, and just a bit for his own pleasure. He saw Esther; she struck him as something out of his line, for he is used to young women who work altar-cloths; he found that Wharton and I liked her; he thought that such material was too good for heathen like us; so he fell in love with her himself and means to turn her into a candlestick of the church. I don't mind. Let him try! He has done what he liked with us all his life. I have worked like a dog for him and his church because he was my friend. Now he will see whether he has met his match. I double you up all round on Esther."

"You men are simply brutal!" said his aunt. "Esther will be an unhappy woman all her life, whether she marries him or not, and you sit there and will not raise a finger to help her."

"Let him convert her, I say;" repeated Strong. "What is your objection to that, aunt Sarah?"

"My objection is that the whole family is only a drove of mules," said Mrs. Murray. "Poor Mr. Hazard does not know what he is undertaking."

"Is Esther very much in love?" asked Strong.

"You know her well enough to know that she would never have accepted him if she were not;" replied Mrs. Murray. "He has hunted her down when she was unhappy, and he is going to make her more unhappy still."

"I guess you're right," said Strong, seriously. "The struggle is going to tear both their poor little hearts out; but what can we do about it? None of us are to blame."

"Ah, George!" exclaimed his aunt. "You are the one most to blame. You should have married Esther yourself, and you had not wit enough to see that while you went dancing round the world, as though such women were plenty as your old fossil toads, the only woman you will ever meet who could have made you happy, was slipping through your fingers, and you hadn't the strength to hold her."

"I own it, aunt Sarah!" said George, and this time he spoke seriously enough to satisfy her. "If I could have fallen in love with Esther and she with me, I believe it would have been better for both of us than that she should marry a high-church parson and I go on digging bones; but some things are too obvious. You can't get a spark without some break in your conductor. I was ready enough to fall in love with Esther, but one can't do that kind of thing in cold blood."

"Well," said Mrs. Murray with a sigh. "You have lost her now, and Mr. Hazard will lose her too. You and he and all your friends are a sort of clever children. We are always expecting you to do something worth doing, and it never comes. You are a sort of water-color, worsted-work, bric-a-brac, washed-out geniuses, just big enough and strong enough to want to do something and never carry it through. I am heartily tired of the whole lot of you, and now I must set to work and get these two girls out of your hands."

"Do you mean to break up this engagement?" asked Strong, who was used to his aunt's criticisms and never answered them.

"The engagement will break itself up," replied his aunt. "It will have to be kept private for a few weeks on account of her father's death and her mourning, and you will see that it never will be announced. If I can, I shall certainly do all in my power to break it up."

"You will?" said Strong. "Well! I mean to do just the contrary. If Esther wants Hazard she shall have him, if I can help her. Why not? Hazard is a good fellow, and will make her a good husband. I have no fault to find with him except that he poaches outside his preserves. He has poached this time to some purpose, but if the parish can stand it, I can."

"The parish cannot stand it," said Mrs. Murray. "They are saying very ugly things already about Esther."

"Then it will not hurt my feelings to see Hazard snub his congregation," replied Strong angrily.

The family conclave ended here, and all parties henceforward fixed their eyes intently on the drama. Mrs. Murray waited with a woman's instinct for her moment to come. Strong tried to counteract her influence by bungling efforts to make the lovers' path smooth. Catherine was a sort of cushion against which all the billiard balls of the game knocked themselves in succession, leaving her cool and elastic temper undisturbed. Three more days passed without throwing much new light on the disputed question whether the engagement could last, except that Esther seemed clearly more anxious and restless. Mr. Hazard was with her several hours every day and watched over her with extreme vigilance. Mrs. Murray took her to drive every afternoon and not a glance of Esther's eyes escaped scrutiny. Strong stopped once or twice at the house but had no chance to interfere until on Thursday morning, his aunt told him that Esther was rapidly getting into a state of mind that must soon bring on a crisis.

"She cannot possibly make it do," said Mrs. Murray. "She is worrying herself to death already. Mr. Hazard ought to see that she can't marry him."

"She will marry him," answered Strong coolly. "Three women out of four think they can't marry a man at first, but when they come to parting with him, they learn better."

"He is passably selfish, your Mr. Hazard. If he thought a little more of his parish, he would not want to put over them a woman like Esther who has not a quality suited to the place."

"Her qualities are excellent," contradicted Strong. "Once in harness she will be kind and gentle, a little tender-mouthed perhaps, and apt to shy at first, but thorough-bred. He is quite right to take her if he can get her, and what does his parish expect to do about it?"

"The first thing they will do about it will be to make Esther miserable. They have begun to gossip already. A young man, even though he is a clergyman, can't be seen always in company with a pretty woman, without exciting remark. Only yesterday I was asked point-blank whether my niece was engaged to Mr. Hazard."

"What did you say?"

"I told a lie of course, all the meaner because it was an equivocation. I said that Mr. Hazard had not honored me with any communication on the subject. I score up this first falsehood to his account."

"If you lie no better than that, Aunt Sarah, Hazard's conscience won't trouble him much. When is the engagement to be out?"

"Very soon, at this rate. I thought that Esther, in common decency, could not announce it for a week or two, but every one already suspects it, and she will have to make it public within another week if she means to do so at all. Now that she is her own mistress and lives by herself, she can't have men so much about the house as she might if her father were living."

"Do you seriously think she will break it off?" asked Strong incredulously.

"I feel surer than ever," answered his aunt. "The criticism is going to be bitter, and the longer Esther waits, the more sharply people will talk. I should not wonder if it ended by driving Mr. Hazard out of the parish. He is not strong enough to shock them much. Then Esther is growing more and more nervous every day because the more she tries to understand, the less she succeeds. Yesterday, when I took her to drive, she was in tears about the atonement, and to-day I suppose she will have gone to bed with a sick headache on account of the Athanasian creed."

"I must talk with her," said Strong. "I think I can make some of those things easier for her."

"You? I thought you laughed at them all."

"So I do, but not because they can't be understood. The trouble is that I think I do understand them. Mystery for mystery science beats religion hollow. I can't open my mouth in my lecture-room without repeating ten times as many unintelligible formulas as ever Hazard is forced to do in his church. I can quiet her mind on that score."

"You had better leave it alone, George! Why should you meddle? Let Mr. Hazard fight his own battles!"

George refused to take this wise advice. He was a tender-hearted fellow and could not bear to see his friends suffer. If Esther loved Hazard and wanted to marry him, she should do so though every dogma of the church stood in her way, and every old woman in the parish shrieked sacrilege. Strong had no respect for the church and no wish to save it trouble, but he believed that Hazard was going blindly under Esther's influence which would sooner or later end by drawing him away from his old forms of belief; and as this was entirely Hazard's affair, if he chose to risk the danger, Strong chose to help him.

"Why not?" said Strong to himself. "It is not a question of earning a living. Both of them are well enough off. If he can turn her into a light of his church, let him do it. If she ends in dragging him out of the church, so much the better. She can't get a better husband, and he can't find a better wife. I mean to see this thing through."

So George strolled round to Esther's house after this interview with his aunt, thinking that he might be able to do good. Being at home there, he went up-stairs unannounced, and finding no one in the library he climbed to the studio, where, on opening the door, he saw Catherine sitting before the fire, looking very much bored. Poor Catherine found it hard to keep up with life in New York. Fresh from the prairie, she had been first saturated with art, and was now plunged in a bottomless ocean of theology. She was glad to see Strong who had in her eyes the advantage of being more practical than the rest of her friends.

"Catherine, how are your sheep?"

"I am glad you have come to look after them," answered Catherine. "I won't be watch-dog much longer. They are too troublesome."

"What mischief are they doing now?"

"Every thing they can think of to worry me. Esther won't eat and can't sleep, and Mr. Hazard won't sleep and can't eat. She tries not to worry him, so she comes down on me with questions and books enough to frighten a professor. Do tell me what to say!"

"Where are your questions?" asked Strong.

"This morning she wanted to know what I thought of apostolic succession. She said she was reading some book by a Dr. Newman. What is apostolic succession?"

"A curious disease, quite common among the poorer classes of Sandwich Islanders," replied Strong. "No one has ever found a cure for it."

"Don't laugh at us! We do nothing but cry now, except when Mr. Hazard is here, and then we pretend to be happy. When Esther cries, I cry too. That makes her laugh. It's our only joke, and we used to have so many."

"Don't you think it rather a moist joke?" asked Strong. "I take mine dry."

"I can't tell what she will think a joke," replied Catherine. "She asked me to-day what was my idea of heaven, and I said it was reading novels in church. She seemed to think this a rich bonanza of a joke, and laughed herself into hysterics, but I was as serious as Mr. Wharton's apostles."

"You are never so funny as when you are serious. Never be so any more! Why don't you get her to paint?"

"She won't. I'm rather glad of it, for if she did, I should have to sit for melancholy, or an angel, or something I'm not fitted for by education."

"What shall we do about it?" asked Strong. "Things can't go on in this way."

"I think the engagement had better come out," said Catherine. "The longer it is kept private, the more she will doubt whether she ought to marry a clergyman. What do you think about marrying clergymen? Wouldn't it almost be better to marry a painter, or even a professor?"

"That would be playing it too low down," replied Strong gravely. "I would recommend you to look out for a swell. What has become of your admirer, Mr. Van Dam?"

"Gone!" said Catherine sadly. "Mr. Wharton and he went off together. There is something about me that scares them all off the ranche."

While they were thus improving each other's minds, the door opened and Esther entered. She was pale and her face had no longer the bright look which Wharton had thought so characteristic, but there was no other sign of trouble about her, and she welcomed her cousin as pleasantly as ever, so that he could hardly believe in the stories he had just heard of her distress.

"Good day, Cousin George," she said. "Thank you for coming to cheer up this poor girl. She needs it. Do take her out and amuse her."

"Come out yourself, Esther. You need it more than she does."

"Aunt Sarah is coming at two o'clock to take me to drive," said Esther. "Catherine hates driving unless she drives herself."

"I thought you hated it too."

"Oh, I hate nothing now," replied Esther, with a little of her old laugh. "I am learning to like every thing."

"Is that in the marriage service?" asked Strong. "Do you have to begin so high up? Couldn't you start easy, and like a few things first,--me for instance--and let the rest wait?"

"No," she said, "you are to come last. Honestly, I am more afraid of you than of all the rest of the world. If you knew what a bug-bear you are to me, you would be afraid of yourself. Don't make fun of me any more! I know I am horribly funny, but you must take me in earnest. Poor papa's last words to me were: 'Laugh and you're safe!'--but if I laugh now, I'm lost."

"This is the first time I ever met any one honest enough to acknowledge that marriage was so sad a thing. Catherine, if I ask you to marry me, will you turn serious?"

"She will turn serious enough if she does it," said Esther. "You would stay with her a week, and then tell her that you were obliged to see a friend in Japan. She would never see you again, but the newspapers would tell her that you had set out to look for bones in the Milky Way."

"What you say sounds to me as though it had a grain of truth," replied Strong. "That reminds me that I got a letter telling me of a lot of new bones only yesterday, but I must leave them underground till the summer; if by that time I can do any thing for you in Oregon, let me know."

"I want you very much to do something for me now," said Esther. "Will you try to be serious a moment for my sake?"

"I don't know," said Strong. "You ask too much all at once. Where are you coming out?"

"Will you answer me a question? Say yes or no!"

"That depends on the question, Mistress Esther! Old birds are not to be caught in old traps. State your question, as we say in the lecture-room."

"Is religion true?"

"I thought so! Cousin Esther, I love you as much as I love any one in this cold world, but I can't answer your question. I can tell you all about the mound-builders or cave-men, so far as known, but I could not tell you the difference between the bones of a saint and those of a heathen. Ask me something easier! Ask me whether science is true!"

"Is science true?"

"No!"

"Then why do you believe in it?"

"I don't believe in it."

"Then why do you belong to it?"

"Because I want to help in making it truer. Now, Esther, just take this matter coolly! You are bothered, I suppose, by the idea that you can't possibly believe in miracles and mysteries, and therefore can't make a good wife for Hazard. You might just as well make yourself unhappy by doubting whether you would make a good wife to me because you can't believe the first axiom in Euclid. There is no science which does not begin by requiring you to believe the incredible."

"Are you telling me the truth?"

"I tell you the solemn truth that the doctrine of the Trinity is not so difficult to accept for a working proposition as any one of the axioms of physics. The wife of my mathematical colleague, to my knowledge, never even stopped to ask whether it was true that a point had neither length, breadth nor thickness."

Esther pondered a few moments, looking into the fire with a grave face. Then she went on:

"You are not talking honestly. Why should I dare tell you that your old fossil bones are a humbug, when I would not for the world talk so to Mr. Hazard? You don't care whether geology is true or not."

"Well, no, not much!" said Strong. "I should care more if you told me that my best Japanese lacquer was modern."

"Besides," said Esther; "you have not answered my question. I want to know what you think, and you won't tell me. Oh! don't let me lose faith in you too! I know your opinions. You think the whole church a piece of superstition. I've heard you say so, and I want you to tell me why. You're my cousin and I've a right to your help, but you won't give it."

"You are a desperate little tyrant," said Strong laughing. "You always were. Do you remember how we fought when we were children because you would have your own way? I used to give in then, but I am old now, and obstinate."

"I know that you always ended by making me go your way," replied Esther; "but that was because I never cared much where I went. Now it is a matter of life and death. I can't move a step, or even let our engagement be announced until I feel sure that I shall not be a load on his neck. Do you think I should hesitate to break it off, even if I broke my heart with it, if I thought it was going to bring trouble on him?"

Against this assault jesting was out of the question. Strong was forced out of this line of defense and found himself in an awkward position. Esther, not outwardly excited, but leaning her chin on her hand, and gazing into the fire with a look of set will, had the calmness of despair. Strong was staggered and hesitated.

"The trouble with you is that you start wrong," said he at length. "You need what is called faith, and are trying to get it by reason. It can't be done. Faith is a state of mind, like love or jealousy. You can never reason yourself into it."

"So Mr. Hazard says," rejoined Esther. "He tells me to wait and it will come, but he wants me to go on just as though I were certain of its coming. I can't wait. If it does not come quickly, I must do something desperate. Now tell me what you would do to get faith if the happiness of your whole life hung on it."

Strong rose uneasily from his seat and stood up before the fire. He began to think himself rash for venturing into this arena. He had always believed his cousin to be stronger than Hazard, because Hazard was a clergyman, but he had not hitherto thought her stronger than himself, and he now looked at her carefully, wondering whether he could have managed her. Never in his life had he felt so nearly in love with her as now, under the temptation to try whether she could be made to give up her will to his. This feeling was the stronger because even in his own eyes his conduct so far seemed a little cowardly and ridiculous. He pulled himself up sharply, and, seeing nothing else to be done, he took up the weapons of the church and asserted the tone of authority.

"Every one who marries," he said, "goes it blind, more or less. If you have faith enough in Hazard to believe in him, you have faith enough to accept his church. Faith means submission. Submit!"

"I want to submit," cried Esther piteously, rising in her turn and speaking in accents of real distress and passion. "Why can't some of you make me? For a few minutes at a time I think it done, and then I suddenly find myself more defiant than ever. I want nothing of the church! Why should it trouble me? Why should I submit to it? Why can't it leave me alone?"

"What you want is the Roman church," continued Strong mercilessly. "They know how to deal with pride of will. Millions of men and women have gone through the same struggle, and the church tells them to fix their eyes on a symbol of faith, and if their eyes wander, scourges them for it." As he talked, he took up the little carved ivory crucifix which stood on the mantel-piece among other bits of studio furniture, and holding it up before her, said: "There! How many people do you think, have come to this Christ of yours that has no meaning to you, and in their struggle with doubt, have pressed it against their hearts till it drew blood? Ask it!"

"Is that all?" said Esther, taking the crucifix from his hand and looking curiously at it. Then she silently put it against her heart and pressed it with more and more force, until Strong caught her hand in alarm and pulled it away.

"Come!" said he coolly, as he forced her to give up the crucifix; "my little bluff has failed. I throw up the hand. You must play it out with Hazard."

Chapter VIII

MR. Hazard was not happy. Like Esther he felt himself getting into a state of mind that threatened to break his spirit. He had been used to ordering matters much as he pleased. His parish at Cincinnati, being his creation, had been managed by him as though he owned it, but at St. John's he found himself less free, and was conscious of incessant criticism. He had been now some months in his new pulpit; his popular success had been marked; St. John's was overflowing with a transient audience, like a theater, to the disgust of regular pew-owners; his personal influence was great; but he felt that it was not yet, and perhaps never could be, strong enough to stand the scandal of his marriage to a woman whose opinions were believed to be radical. On this point he was not left in doubt, for the mere suspicion of his engagement raised a little tempest in the pool. The stricter sect, not without reason, were scandalized. They held to their creed, and the bare mention of Esther Dudley's name called warm protests from their ranks. They flatly said that it would be impossible for Mr. Hazard to make them believe his own doctrine to be sound, if he could wish to enter into such a connection. None but a free-thinker could associate with the set of free-thinkers, artists and other unusual people whose society Mr. Hazard was known to affect, and his marriage to one of them would give the unorthodox a hold on the parish which would end by splitting it.

One of his strongest friends, who had done most to bring him to New York and make his path pleasant, came to him with an account of what was said and thought, softening the expression so as to bear telling.

"You ought to hear about it," said he, "so I tell you; but it is between you and me. I don't ask whether you are engaged to Miss Dudley. For my own pleasure, I wish you may be. If I were thirty years younger I would try for her myself; but we all know that she has very little more religious experience than a white rosebud. I'm not strict myself, I don't mind a little looseness on the creed, but the trouble is that every old woman in the parish knows all about the family. Her father, William Dudley, a great friend of mine as you know, was a man who liked to defy opinion and never hid his contempt for ours. He paid for a pew at St. John's because, he said, society needs still that sort of police. But he has told me a dozen times that he could get more police for his money by giving it to the Roman Catholics. He never entered his pew. His brother-in-law Murray is just as bad, never goes near the church, and is always poking fun at us who do. The professor is a full-fledged German Darwinist, and believes in nothing that I know of, unless it is himself. Esther took to society, and I'm told by my young people that she was one of the best waltzers in town until she gave it up for painting and dinners. Her set never bothered their heads about the church. Of the whole family, Mrs. Murray is the only one who has any weight in the parish, and she has a good deal, but if I know her, she won't approve the match any more than the rest, and you must expect to get the reputation of being unorthodox. Only yesterday old Tarbox told me he thought you were rather weak on the Pentateuch, and the best I could say was that now-a-days we must choose between weak doctrines and weak brains, and of the two, I preferred to let up on the Pentateuch."

All this was the more annoying to Mr. Hazard because his orthodoxy was his strong point. Like most vigorous-minded men, seeing that there was no stopping-place between dogma and negation, he preferred to accept dogma. Of all weaknesses he most disliked timid and half-hearted faith. He would rather have jumped at once to Strong's pure denial, than yield an inch to the argument that a mystery was to be paltered with because it could not be explained. The idea that these gossiping parishioners of his should undertake to question his orthodoxy, tried his temper. He knew that they disliked his intimacy with artists and scientific people, but he was not afraid of his parish, and meant that his parish should be a little afraid of him. He preferred to give them some cause of fault-finding in order to keep them awake. His greatest annoyance came from another side. If such gossip should reach Esther's ears, it would go far towards driving her beyond his control, and he knew that even without this additional alarm, it was with the greatest difficulty he could quiet and restrain her. The threatened disaster was terrible enough when looked at as a mere question of love, but it went much deeper. He was ready to override criticism and trample on remonstrance if he could but succeed in drawing her into the fold, because his lifelong faith, that all human energies belonged to the church, was on trial, and, if it broke down in a test so supreme as that of marriage, the blow would go far to prostrate him forever. What was his religious energy worth if it did not carry him successfully through such stress, when the strongest passion in life was working on its side?

At the hour when Strong was making his disastrous attempt to relieve Esther of her scruples, Mr. Hazard was listening to these exasperating criticisms from his parish. It was his habit to come every day at noon to pass an hour with Esther, and as he entered the house to-day he met Strong leaving it, and asked him to spare the time for a talk the same evening. He wanted Strong's advice and help.

A brace of lovers in lower spirits than Hazard and Esther could not have been easily found in the city of New York or its vicinity this day, and the worst part of their depression was that each was determined to hide it from the other. Esther could not tell him much more than he already knew, and would not throw away her charm over him by adding to his anxieties, while he knew that any thing he could tell her would add to her doubts and perhaps drive her to some sudden and violent step. Luckily they were too much attached to each other to feel the full awkwardness of their attitude.

"It is outrageously pleasant to be with you," he said. "One's conscience revolts against such enjoyment. I wonder whether I should ever get enough."

"I shall never give you a chance," said she. "I shall be strict with you and send you off to your work before you can get tired of me."

"You make me shockingly weary of my work," he answered. "At times I wish I could stop making a labor of religion, and enjoy it a little. How pleasant it would be to go off to Japan together and fill our sketch-books with drawings."

This suggestion came on Esther so suddenly that she forgot herself and gave a little cry of delight. "Oh, are you in earnest?" she said. "It seems to me that I could crawl and swim there if you would go with me."

Then she saw her mistake. Her outburst of pleasure gave him pain. He was displeased with himself for speaking so thoughtlessly, for this idea of escape made both of them conscious of the chasm on whose edge they stood.

"No, I wish I could be in earnest," he answered, "but I have just begun work, and there is no vacation for me. You must keep up my courage. Without your help I shall break down."

If he had thought out in advance some device for distressing her, he could not have succeeded better. She had just time to realize the full strength of her love for him, when he thrust the church between them, and bade her love him for its sake. The delight of wandering through the world by his side flashed on her mind only to show a whole Fifth Avenue congregation as her rival. The conviction that the church was hateful to her and that she could never trust herself to obey or love it, forced itself on her at the very moment when she felt that life was nothing without her lover, and that to give up all the world besides in order to go with him, would be the only happiness she cared to ask of her destiny. The feeling was torture. So long as he remained she controlled it, but when he went away she wrung her hands in despair and asked herself again and again what she could do; whether she was not going mad with the strain of these emotions.

Before she had fairly succeeded in calming herself, her aunt came to take her out for their daily drive. Since her father's death, this drive with her aunt, or a walk with Catherine, had been her only escape from the confinement of the house, and she depended on it more than on food and drink. They went first to some shops where Mrs. Murray had purchases to make, and Esther sat alone in the carriage while her aunt was engaged within in buying whatever household articles were on her list for the day. As Esther, sitting quietly in the corner of the carriage, mechanically watched the passers-by, she saw the familiar figure of Mr. Wharton among them, and, with a sudden movement of her old vivacity, she bent forward, caught his eye, and held out her hand. He stopped before the carriage window, and spoke with more than common cordiality.

"I wanted to come and see you, but I heard you received no one."

"I will always see you," she replied.

Looking more than ever shy and embarrassed he said that he should certainly come as soon as his work would let him, and meanwhile he wanted her to know how glad he was to be able at last to offer his congratulations.

"Congratulations? On what?" said she, beginning to flush scarlet.

Wharton stammered out: "I was this moment told by a lady of your acquaintance that your engagement to Mr. Hazard was formally announced to-day."

Esther grew as pale as she had been red, and answered quietly: "When my engagement to any one is announced, I promise to let you know of it, Mr. Wharton, before the world knows it."

He apologized and passed on. Esther, shrinking back into her corner, struggled in vain to recover from this new blow. Mrs. Murray, on returning, found her in a state of feverish excitement.

"I am being dragged in against my will," said she. "I am beyond my depth. What am I to do?"

"Most women feel so at first," replied her aunt calmly. "Many want to escape. Some are afterwards sorry they didn't."

"Have you heard of this too, and not told me?" asked Esther.

Mrs. Murray had thought too long over the coming trouble to hesitate now that the moment had come. She had watched for the crisis; her mind was made up to take her share of the responsibility; so she now settled herself down to the task. As the thing had to be done, she thought that the shortest agony was the most merciful.

"Yes!" she answered. "Several persons have mentioned it to me, and I have had to profess not to know what they meant."

"What did they say?" asked Esther breathlessly.

"The only one who has talked openly to me about it is your friend Mrs. Dyer. The story came from her, and I believe she invented it. Of course she disapproves. I never knew her to approve."

"What reason does she give?"

"She says that you are an amiable girl, but one given up to worldly pursuits and without a trace of religious principle; the last woman to make a clergyman's wife, though you might do very well for an artist or somebody wicked enough for you, as I gathered her idea. I am told that she amuses herself by adding that she never took Mr. Hazard for a clergyman, and the sooner he quits the pulpit, the better. She is never satisfied without hitting every one she can reach."

"What does she want?" asked Esther.

"I suppose she wants to break off the intimacy. She thinks there is no actual engagement yet, and the surest way to prevent one is to invent one in time."

Esther reflected a few minutes before beginning again.

"Aunt, do you think I am fit to be his wife?"

"It all depends on you," replied Mrs. Murray. "If you feel yourself fit, you are the best person in the world for it. You would be a brand saved from the burning, and it will be a great feather in Mr. Hazard's cap to convert you into a strong church-woman. He could then afford to laugh at Mrs. Dyer, and all the parish would laugh with him."

"Aunt!" said Esther in an awe-struck tone; "I am jealous of the church. I never shall like it."

"Then, Esther, you are doing very wrong to let Mr. Hazard think you can marry him. You will ruin him, and yourself too."

"He has seen how I have struggled," answered Esther with a sort of sob. "I never knew how gentle and patient a man could be until I saw how he helped me. He began by taking all the risk. I told him faithfully that I was not fit for him, and he said that he only asked me to love him. I did love him. I love him so much that if he were a beggar in the street here and wanted me, I would get down and pick up rags with him."

She moaned out this last sentence so piteously that Mrs. Murray's heart bled. "Poor child!" she thought. "It is like crushing a sparrow with a stone. I must do it quickly."

"Tell him all about it, Esther! It is his affair more than yours. If his love is great enough to take you as you are, do your best, and never let him repent it; but you must make him choose between you and his profession."

"I can't do that!" said Esther quickly. "I would rather go on and leave it all to chance."

"If you do," replied Mrs. Murray, "You will only put yourself into his hands. Sooner or later Mr. Hazard must find out that you don't belong to him. Then it will be his duty to make you choose between your will and his. You had better not let yourself be put in such a position. A woman can afford to break an engagement, but she can't afford to be thrown over by a man, not even if he is a clergyman, and that is what Mr. Hazard will have to do to you if you let him go on."

"Oh, I know him better!" broke out Esther. She resented bitterly this cruel charge against her lover, but nevertheless it cut into her quivering nerves until her love seemed to wither under it. The idea that he could ever want to get rid of her was the last drop in her cup of bitterness. Mrs. Murray knew how to crush her sparrow. She needed barely five minutes to do it. From the moment that Esther's feminine pride was involved, the sparrow was dead.

Certainly Hazard had as yet no thought of giving up his prize, but he had reached the first stage of wondering what he should do with it. Naturally sanguine and perhaps a little spoiled by flattery and success, he had taken for granted that Esther would at once absorb her existence in his. He hoped that she would become, like most converts, more zealous than himself. After a week of trial, finding her not only unaffected by his influence but actually slipping more and more from his control, he began to feel an alarm which grew more acute every hour, and brought him for the first time face to face with the possibility of failure. What could he do to overcome this fatal coldness.

With very uneasy feelings he admitted that a step backwards must be taken, and it was for this purpose that he wanted to consult with Strong. Never was the Church blessed with a stranger ally than this freest of free thinkers, who looked at churches very much as he would have looked at a layer of extinct oysters in a buried mud-bank. Strong's notion was that since the Church continued to exist, it probably served some necessary purpose in human economy, though he could himself no more understand the good of it than he could comprehend the use of human existence in any shape. Since men and women were here, idiotic and purposeless as they might be, they had what they chose to call a right to amuse themselves in their own way, and if this way made some happy without hurting others, Strong was ready enough to help. He was as willing to help Hazard as to help Esther, provided the happiness of either seemed to be within reach; and as for forms of faith it seemed to him as easy to believe one thing as another. If Esther believed any thing at all, he could see no reason why she might not believe whatever Hazard wanted.

With all the good-will in the world he came from his club after dinner to Hazard's house. As the way was short he did not even grumble, knowing that he could smoke his cigar as well at one place as at the other. He found Hazard in his library, walking up and down, with more discouragement on his face than Strong had ever seen there before. The old confusion of the room had not quite disappeared; the books were not yet all arranged on their shelves; pictures still leaned against the wall; dust had accumulated on them, and even on the large working table where half-written sermons lay scattered among a mass of notes, circulars, invitations and unanswered letters. It was clear that Mr. Hazard was not an orderly person and needed nothing so much as a wife. Esther would have been little flattered at the remark, now rather common among his older friends, that almost any wife would be better for him than none.

With an echo of his old boyish cordiality he welcomed Strong, gave him the best easy-chair by the fire, and told him to smoke as much as he liked.

"Perhaps a cigar will give you wisdom," he added. "You will need it, for I want to consult you about Esther."

"Don't!" said Strong laconically.

"Hush!" replied Hazard. "You put me out. I don't consult you because I like it, but because I must. The matter is becoming serious, and I must either consult you or Mrs. Murray. I prefer to begin with you. It's a habit I have."

"At your own risk, then!"

"I suppose I shall have to take whatever risk there is in it," answered Hazard. "I must do something, for if my amiable parishioner, Mrs. Dyer, gets at Esther in her present state of mind, the poor child will work herself into a brain fever. But first tell me one thing! Were you ever in love with Esther yourself!"

"Never!" replied Strong, peacefully. "Esther always told me that I had nothing but chalk and plate-glass in my mind, and could never love or be loved. We have discussed it a good deal. She says I am an old glove that fits well enough but will not cling. Of course it was her business to make me cling and I told her so. No! I never was in love with her, but I have been nearer it these last ten days than ever before. She will come out of her trouble either made or marred, and a year hence I will tell you which."

"Take care," said Hazard. "I have learned to conquer all my passions except jealousy, and that I have never yet tried."

"If she marries you," replied Strong, "that will settle it."

"*If* she marries me!" broke out Hazard, paying no attention to Strong's quiet assumption that for Esther to be thus married was to be marred. "Do you mean that there is any doubt about it?"

"I supposed that was what you wanted to talk about," answered Strong with some surprise. "Is any thing else the matter?"

"You always put facts in a horribly materialistic way," responded Hazard. "I wanted to consult you about making things easier for her, not about broken engagements."

"Bless your idealistic soul!" said Strong. "I have already tried to help her in that way, and made a shocking piece of work. Has not Esther told you?" and he went on to give his friend an account of the morning's conversation in which his attempt to preach the orthodox faith had suffered disastrous defeat. Hazard listened closely, and at the end sat for some time silent in deep thought. Then he said:

"Esther told me something of this, though I did not get the idea it was so serious. I am glad to know the whole; but you should not have tried to discipline her. Leave the thunders of the church to me."

"What could I do?" asked Strong. "She jammed me close up to the wall. I did not know where to turn. You would have been still less pleased if I had done what she wanted, and given her the whole Agnostic creed."

"I am not quite so sure about that," rejoined Hazard thoughtfully. "I am never afraid of pure atheism; it is the flabby kind of sentimental deism that annoys me, because it is as slippery as air. If you will tell her honestly what your skepticism means, I will risk the consequences."

"Just as you like!" said Strong; "if she attacks me again, I will give her the strongest kind of a dose of what you are pleased to call pure atheism. Not that I mind what it is called. She shall have it crude. Only remember that I prefer to tackle her on the other side."

"Do as you please!" said Hazard. "Now let us come to business. All Esther wants is time. I am as certain as I can be of any thing in this uncertain world, that a few weeks, or at the outside a few months, will quiet all her fears. What I want is to stop this immediate strain which is enough to distract any woman."

"Stop the strain of course!" said Strong. "I want to stop it almost as much as you do, but it looked to me this morning as though what you call strain were a steady drift which pays no sort of heed to our trying to stop it."

"I feel sure it is only nervousness," said Hazard earnestly. "Give her time, quiet and rest! She will come out right."

"Then what is it that I can do?"

"Help me to get her out of New York."

"I will ask my aunt to help you," replied Strong; "but how are we to do it? The earthly paradise is not to be found in this neighborhood in the middle of February."

"Never mind! If you and she will back me, we can do it, and it must be done instantly to be of use. There is no end of parish gossip which must not come to Esther's ears, or it will drive her wild. Take her to Florida, California, or even to Europe if you can! Give me time to smooth things down! If she stays here we shall all be the worse for it."

As usual, Hazard had his way. George consented to do all he asked and even to take Esther away himself if it were necessary. The next morning he appeared soon after breakfast at his aunt's to report Hazard's wishes and to devise the means of satisfying them. Much to his relief, and rather to his astonishment, he found Mrs. Murray disposed to look with favor on the idea. She listened quietly to his story, and after a little reflection, asked:

"Where do you think we had best go?"

"Do you mean to go too?" asked Strong in surprise. "Why should you tear yourself up by the roots to please Hazard?"

"Those two girls can't go alone," said Mrs. Murray; "and as for me, I don't go to please Mr. Hazard. I don't think he is going to be pleased."

"Now what mischief are you brewing, Aunt Sarah? I am Hazard's friend, and bound to see him through. Don't make me a party to any scheme against him!"

"You are not very bright, George, and just now you are rather ridiculous, because you do not in the least know what you are about."

"Go on!" said Strong with irrepressible good nature. "Play out all your trumps and let my suit in!"

"Could you be ready to start for Niagara by to-morrow morning?" asked his aunt.

"To-morrow is Saturday. Yes! I could manage it."

"Could you get some pleasant man to go with you?"

"Not much chance!" he replied. "I might ask Wharton, but he is very busy."

"Try for him! I will send you a note to your club early this evening to say whether I shall want you or not. If I make you go, I shall go too, and take Esther and Catherine."

"I will do any thing you want," said Strong, "on condition that you tell me what you are about."

Mrs. Murray looked at her nephew with a pitying air, and said:

"Any one with common sense might see that Esther's engagement never could come to any thing."

"But you are trying to hold her to it."

"I am trying to do no such thing. I expect Esther to dismiss him; then she will need some change of scene, and I mean to take her away."

"To-day?" asked Strong in alarm.

"To-day or to-morrow! Sooner or later! We have got to be ready for it at any moment. Now do you understand?"

"I think I am beginning to catch on," replied Strong with a grave face. "I wish I were out of the scrape."

"I told you never to get into it," rejoined his aunt.

"Poor Hazard!" muttered George, wondering whether he could do anything to ward off this last blow from his friend.

Even as he spoke, the crisis was at hand. Mrs. Murray's calculations were exact. While Hazard had been arranging with Strong the plan for getting Esther away from New York, letting the engagement remain private, Esther, in a state of feverish restlessness was wearying Catherine with endless discussion of her trouble. Even Catherine felt that, one way or the other, it was time for this thing to stop. Esther had passed the stage of self-submission, and was in a mutinous mood. She had given up the effort to reconcile herself with her situation, and yet could talk of nothing but Hazard, until Catherine's good-nature was sorely tried.

"I never was such a bore till now," said Esther at length, as though she could not at all understand it. "I could sometimes be quite pleasant. I used to go about the house singing and laughing. Am I going mad?"

"Suppose we go mad together?" said Catherine. "I will if you will."

"Suppose we elope together!" said Esther. "Will you run off with me?"

"Any where but to Colorado," replied Catherine, "I have seen all I want of Colorado."

"We will take our wedding journey together and leave our husbands behind.

Let them catch us if they can!" continued Esther, talking rapidly and feverishly.

"It would be rather fun to see Mr. Hazard driving Mr. Van Dam's fast trotters after us," remarked Catherine.

"When shall we go? Can we start now?"

"Don't you think we had better go to bed just now, and elope in the morning?" grumbled Catherine. "They can see us better by daylight."

"I tell you, Catherine, that I am in awful earnest. I mean to go away somewhere, and if you won't go with me, I shall go alone."

"Suppose they catch us?" said Catherine.

"I don't care! I am hopelessly wicked! I can't be respectable and believe the thirty-nine articles. I can't go to church every Sunday or hold my tongue or pretend to be pious."

"Then why don't you tell him so, and let him run away?" asked Catherine.

"Because then he would think it his duty to run," said Esther, "and I don't want to be run away from. Would you like to have the world think you were jilted?"

"How you do torture your poor brain!" said Catherine pityingly. "There! Go to bed now! It is long past midnight. To-morrow I will run you off, and you never shall go to church any more."

Esther was really in a way to alarm her friends. She went to bed as Catherine advised, but her sleep was feverish, as though she had dieted herself on opium. She acted over and over again the scene that lay before her, until her brain felt physically weary, as though it had run all night round and round its narrow chamber. Her head was so tired in the morning that it was a relief to get up and face real life. She dressed herself with uncommon care. She meant to keep her crown even though she threw away her kingdom, and though she should lose a husband, she intended to hold fast her lover. Women have the right to this coquetry with fate. Iphigenia herself, when the priests, who muffled her voice, stretched her on the altar and struck the knife in her throat, tried to charm them with her sad eyes while her saffron blood was flowing, and they saw that she would have charmed them with her voice even when hope had vanished.

The unfortunate Hazard was not precisely an Agamemnon, and would have liked nothing better than to stop the sacrifice which seemed to him much too closely like a triumph over himself. His own throat was the one which felt itself in closest danger of the knife. At noon, as usual, he came in, trying to conceal his anxiety under an appearance of confidence, but Esther's first words routed all his forces and drove him back to his last defense.

"I should not have let you come to-day. I ought to have written to bid you good-by, but it was too hard not to see you once more. I am going away."

"I am going with you," said Hazard quietly.

"No, you are not!" replied Esther. "You are to stay here and attend to your duties. Forget me as soon as you can."

Hazard took this address very good-naturedly, and neither showed nor felt surprise. "You have been tormented by this idea," he said, "and I am glad now to meet it face to face. For us to part is impossible. You and I are one. You cannot get yourself apart from me, though you may make us both unhappy; and even if you go away forever you will still belong to me. I could not release you if I would."

"I don't want to be released," said Esther. "If it were only for that, I would stay with you as long as you would let me. I would do whatever you told me, and never ask a question. But I will not be your evil genius. I will be your good genius or nothing."

"Be my good genius then! What stands in your way?"

"I have tried and failed. Already there is not a woman in your parish who is not saying that I shall ruin you and your career. I would rather die than run the risk of your thinking I had done you harm."

"If I, seeing all this, am willing to take the risk, why should you ally yourself against me with all the petty gossip of a parish?" asked Hazard. "Such talk will stop the moment you say the word. Let me go out now and announce our engagement! If I did not sometimes shock my parish, I could never manage them."

"But I would rather not be made useful in that way," said Esther with a momentary gleam of humor in her eyes. "No woman wants to be shocking. Now I have a favor to ask of you. It is the last, and I want you to promise to grant it."

"Not if it is to give you up."

"I want you to make it easy for me. I am trying to do right. I am so weak and unhappy after all that has happened that if you are cruel to me, I shall want to die. Be generous! You know I am right. Let me go quietly, and do not torture me!"

She sat down as they were talking. He, sinking into a chair by her side, took both her hands in his, and she did not try to free them. When she made her appeal, he answered as quietly and stubbornly as before: "Never! You are my wife, and my wife you will always be in my eyes. I shall not give you up. I shall not make it easy for you to give me up. I shall make it as hard as I can. I shall prevent it. But I will do anything you like to make our engagement easy, and I came to-day with something to propose."

No doubt, had Hazard taken her at her word and coolly walked away, Esther would have been very unpleasantly surprised. She did not expect him to obey her first orders, nor did she want to hurry the moment of separation, or to part from him with a feeling of bitterness. His presence always soothed and satisfied her, and she had never been calmer than now, when, with her hands in his, she waited for his new suggestion.

"I want you to do me a favor not nearly so great as the one you ask of me," said he. "Give me time! Go abroad, if you think best, but let our engagement stand! Let me come out and join you in the summer. I am ready to see you go where you like, and stay as long as you please, if you take me with you."

Esther reflected for a moment how she should answer. She had thought of this plan and rejected it long before, because it seemed to her to combine all possible objections, and to get rid of none. She knew that neither six months nor six years would make her a fit wife for Hazard, and that it would be dishonest to lure him on by any hope that she could change her nature; but it was not easy to put this in delicate words. At length she answered simply.

"I am almost the last person in the world whom you ought to marry. Time will only make me more unfit."

"Should you think so," he asked quickly, "if I were a lawyer, or a stock broker?"

She colored and withdrew her hands. "No!" she said. "If you were a stock broker I suppose I should be quite satisfied. Now I am low enough, am I not? Don't make me feel more degraded than I am. Let me go off alone and forget me!"

But Hazard continued to press his point with infinite patience and gentle obstinacy, until her powers of resistance were almost worn out. Again and again the tears came into her eyes, and she would have told him gladly to take her and do what he liked with her, if she had not steeled herself with the fixed thought that in this case the whole struggle must begin again, and he would know no better what to do with her than before. He would talk only of their love, attacking her where she could not defend herself, and took almost a pleasure in acknowledging that she was at his mercy.

"Oh, if you want only my love," she said at last with a gesture of despair, "I have lost all my pride. I would like nothing better than to lie down and die in your arms. I will promise to be faithful to you all my life; to go into a convent if you want it; to drown myself, or do any thing but lose your love."

"It is not so very much I ask," he urged. "You fear hurting me by marrying me. Do you ever reflect how much you will hurt me by refusing? Do you know how solitary I am? Not a human being counts for any thing in my life. When I go to my rooms, I am terrified to think how lonely they will seem unless I can keep you in my mind. You are the only woman I ever loved. You are my companion, my ideal, my life. We two souls have wandered about the universe from all eternity waiting to meet each other, and now after we have met and become one, you try to part us."

As he went on with this appeal, he wrought himself into stronger and stronger expression of feeling, while Esther fell back in her chair and covered her face with her hands.

"If I am willing to risk every thing for you, why should you refuse to grant me so small a favor as I ask? Look, Esther! What more can I do? Will you not make a little sacrifice of pride for me? Will you ever find another man to love you as I do?"

"How merciless you are!" sobbed Esther.

"I ask only for time," he hurried on. "To part from you now, in this room, at this moment, forever, is awful! You may go if you will, but I shall follow you. I will never give you up. You are mine--mine--mine!"

His passionate cry of love was more than flesh and blood could bear. With an uncontrollable impulse of self-abandonment Esther held out her hand to him and he seized her in his arms, kissing her passionately again and again, till she tore herself away.

"There, go!" said she, breathlessly. "Go! You are killing me!"

Without waiting an answer, she turned and hurried away to her room, where, flinging herself down, she sobbed till her hysterical passion wore itself out.

Chapter IX

AT her usual hour for taking Esther to drive, Mrs. Murray appeared at the house, where she found Catherine looking as little pleased as though she were ordered to return to her native prairie.

"We have sent him off," said she, "and we are clean broke up."

The tears were in her eyes as she thus announced the tragedy which had been acted only an hour or two before, but her coolness more than ever won Mrs. Murray's heart.

"Tell me all that has happened," said she.

"I've told you all I know," replied Catherine. "They had it out here for an hour or more, and then Esther ran up to her room. I've been to the door half a dozen times, and could hear her crying and moaning inside."

Mrs. Murray sat down with a rueful face and a weary sigh, but there was no sign of hesitation or doubt in her manner. The time had come for her to take command, and she did it without fretfulness or unnecessary words.

"You are the only person I know with a head," said she to Catherine. "You have some common sense and can help me. I want to take Esther out of this place within six hours. Can you manage to get every thing ready?"

"I will run it all if you will take care of Esther," replied Catherine. "I'm not old enough to boss her."

"All you will have to do is to see that your trunks are packed for a week's absence and you are both ready to start by eight o'clock," answered Mrs. Murray. "Do you attend to that and I will look out for the rest. Now wait here a few minutes while I go up and see Esther!"

Catherine wished nothing better than to start any where at the shortest notice. She was tired of the long strain on her sympathies and feelings, and was glad to be made useful in a way that pleased her practical mind. Mrs. Murray went up to Esther's room. All was quiet inside. The storm had spent itself. Knowing that her aunt would come, Esther had made the effort to be herself again, and when Mrs. Murray knocked at the door, the voice that told her to come in was firm and sweet as ever. Esther was getting ready for her drive, and though her eyes, in spite of bathing, were red and swollen, they had no longer the anxious and troubled look of a hunted creature which had so much alarmed Mrs. Murray for the last few days. Her expression was more composed than it had been for weeks. Her love had already become a sorrow rather than a passion, and she would not, for a world of lovers, have gone back to the distress of yesterday.

Mrs. Murray took in the whole situation at a glance and breathed a breath of relief. At length the crisis was past and she had only to save the girl from brooding over her pain. Without waiting for an explanation, she plunged into the torrent of Esther's woes.

"Mr. Murray and I are going to Niagara by the night train. I want you and Catherine to go with us."

"You are an angel!" answered Esther. "Did Catherine tell you how I wanted to run away! You knew it would be so? I will go any where; the further the better; but how can I drag you and poor Uncle John away from town at this season? Can't I go off alone with Catherine?"

"Nonsense!" said her aunt briefly. "I shall be glad to get away from New York. I am tired of it. Get your trunks packed! Put in your sketching materials, and we will pick you up at eight o'clock. George shall come on to-morrow and pass Sunday with us."

Esther thanked her aunt with effusion. "I am going to show you how well I can behave. Uncle John shall not know that any thing is the matter with me unless you tell him. I won't be contemptible, even if I have got red eyes."

Not five minutes were needed to decide on the new departure. Esther and Catherine found relief and amusement in the bustle of preparation. If Esther was still a little feverish and excited, she was able to throw it off in work. She was no longer an object of pity; it was her uncle and aunt who deserved deepest compassion. What worse shock was possible for an elderly, middle-aged New York lawyer than to return to his house at six o'clock and find that he is to have barely time for his dinner and cigar before being thrust out into the cold and hideous darkness of a February night, in order to travel some four hundred miles through a snow-bound country? It is true that he had received some little warning to arrange his affairs for an absence over Saturday, but at best the blow was a severe one, and he bore it with a silent fortitude which wrung his wife's heart. She was a masterful mistress, but she was good to those who obeyed, and she even showed the weakness of begging him not to go, although in her soul she knew that he must.

"After all, John, you needn't go with us. I can take the girls alone."

"As I understand it, you have engaged my professional services," he replied. "On the whole I prefer prevention to cure. I would rather help Esther to run away, than get her a divorce."

"When I am dead, you shall stay quietly at home and be perfectly happy," she answered, with the venerable device which wives, from earliest history, have used to palliate their own sins.

Nevertheless he felt almost as miserable as his wife, when, wrapped in cloaks and rugs, they left their bright dining room and shuffled down the steps into the outside darkness to their carriage. He expressed opinions about lovers which would have put a quick end to the human race had they been laws of nature. He wished the church would take them all and consign them to its own favorite place of punishment. He had a disagreeable trick of gibing at his wife's orthodoxy on this point, and when she remonstrated at his profanity, he smiled contentedly and said: "There is nothing profane about it. It is sound church doctrine, and I envy you for being able to believe it. You can hope to see them with your own eyes getting their reward, confound them!"

Consoling himself with this pleasing hope, they started off, and in five minutes were at Esther's door. After taking the two girls into the carriage, Mr. Murray became more affable and even gay. By the time the party was established in their sleeping car, he had begun to enjoy himself. He had too often made such journeys, and was too familiar with every thing on the road to be long out of humor, and for once it was amusing to have a pair of pretty girls to take with him. Commonly his best society was some member of the Albany Legislature, and his only conversation was about city charters and railroad legislation. The variety had its charm. Esther was as good as her word. She made a desperate battle to recover her gayety, and the little excitement of a night journey helped the triumph of her pride. Determined that she would not be an object of pity, she made the most of all her chances, pretended to take in earnest her uncle's humorous instructions as to the art of arranging a sleeping berth, and horrified her aunt by letting him induce Catherine and herself to eat hot doughnuts and mince pies on the train. It was outwardly a gay little party which rattled along the bank of the snowy river on their way northward.

The gayety, it is true, was forced. For the first ten minutes Esther felt excited by the sense of flight and the rapid motion which was carrying her she knew not where,--away into the infinite and unknown. What lay before her, beyond the darkness of the moment, she hardly cared. Never again could she go back to the old life, but like a young bird that has lost its mate, she must fly on through the gloom till it end. Unluckily all her thoughts brought her back to Hazard. Even this sense of resembling a bird that flies, it knows not where, recalled to her the sonnet of Petrarch which she had once translated for him, and which, since then, had been always on his lips, although she had never dreamed that it could have such meaning to her. Long after she had established herself in her berth, solitary and wakeful, the verses made rhythm with the beat of the car-wheels:

"Vago augelletto che cantando vai!"

They were already far on their way, flying up the frozen stream of the Hudson, before she was left alone with her thoughts in the noisy quiet of the rushing train. She could not even hope to sleep. Propping herself up against the pillows, she raised the curtain of her window and stared into the black void outside. Nothing in nature could be more mysterious and melancholy than this dark, polar world, beside which a winter storm on the Atlantic was at least exciting. On the ocean the forces of nature have it their own way; nothing comes between man and the elements; but as Esther gazed out into the night, it was not the darkness, or the sense of cold, or the vagrant snow-flakes driving against the window, or the heavy clouds drifting through the sky, or even the ghastly glimmer and reflection of the snow-fields, that, by contrast, made the grave seem cheerful; it was rather the twinkling lights from distant and invisible farm-houses, the vague outlines of barn-yards and fences along doubtful roads, the sudden flash of lamps as the train hurried through unknown stations, or the unfamiliar places where it stopped, while the tap-tap of the trainmen's hammers on the wheels beneath sounded like spirit-rappings. These signs of life behind the veil were like the steady lights of shore to the drowning fisherman off the reef outside. Every common-place kerosene lamp whose rays struggled from distant, snow-clad farms, brought a picture of peace and hope to Esther. Not one of these invisible roofs but might shelter some realized romance, some contented love. In so dark and dreary a world, what a mad act it was to fly from the only happiness life offered! What a strange idea to seek safety by refusing the only protection worth having! Love was all in all! Esther had never before felt herself so helpless as in the face of this outer darkness, and if her lover had now been there to claim her, she would have dropped into his arms as unresistingly as a tired child.

As the night wore on, the darkness and desolation became intolerable, and she shut them out, only to find herself suffocated by the imprisonment of her sleeping-berth. Hour after hour dragged on; the little excitement of leaving Albany was long past, and the train was wandering through the dullness of Central New York, when at last a faint suspicion of dim light appeared in the landscape, and Esther returned to her window. If any thing could be drearier than the blackness of night, it was the grayness of dawn, which had all the cold terror of death and all the grim repulsiveness of life joined in an hour of despair. Esther could now see the outlines of farm-houses as the train glided on; snow-laden roofs and sheds; long stretches of field with fences buried to their top rails in sweeping snow-drifts; in the houses, lights showed that toil had begun again; smoke rose from the chimneys; figures moved in the farm-yards; a sleigh could be seen on a decided road; the world became real, prosaic, practical, mechanical, not worth struggling about; a mere colorless, passionless, pleasureless grayness. As the mystery vanished, the pain passed and the brain grew heavy. Esther's eyelids drooped, and she sank at last into a sleep so sound that there was hardly need for Catherine to stand sentry before her berth and frown the car into silence. The sun was high above the horizon; the sky was bright and blue; the snowy landscape flashed with the sparkle of diamonds, when Esther woke, and it was with a cry of pleasure that she felt her spirits answer the sun.

Meanwhile her flight was no secret. As the train that carried her off drew out of the great station into the darkness for its long journey of three thousand miles, two notes were delivered to gentlemen only a few squares away. Strong at his club received one from Mrs. Murray: "We all start for Clifton at nine o'clock. Come to-morrow and bring a companion if you can. We need to be amused." The Reverend Stephen Hazard received the other note, which was still more brief, but long enough to strike him with panic; for it contained two words: "Good-by! Esther."

No sooner did Strong receive his missive than he set himself in active motion. Wharton, who commonly dined at the club, was so near that Strong had only to pass the note over to him. Whether Wharton was still suffering from the shock of his wife's appearance, or disappearance, or whether he was on the look-out for some chance to see again his friend Catherine, or whether he found it pleasanter to take a holiday than to attack his long arrears of work, the idea of running up to Niagara for Sunday happened to strike him as pleasant, and he promised to join Strong at the Erie Station in the morning. Strong knew him too well to count on his keeping the engagement, but could do no more, and they both left the club to make their preparations. Strong had another duty. Before stirring further, he must talk with Hazard. The affair was rapidly taking a shape that might embarrass them both.

Going directly to Hazard's house, he burst into the library, where he found his friend trying to work in spite of the heavy load on his mind. Throwing him Mrs. Murray's note, Strong waited without a word while Hazard read it more eagerly than though it had been a summons to a bishopric. The mysterious good-by, which had arrived but a few minutes before, had upset his nerves, and at first the note which Strong brought reassured him, for he thought that Mrs. Murray was earning out his own wishes and drawing Esther nearer to him.

"Then we have succeeded!" he cried.

"Not much!" said Strong dryly. "It is a genuine flight and escape in all the forms. You are out-generaled and your line of attack is left all in the air."

"I shall follow!" said Hazard, doggedly.

"No good! They are in earnest," replied Strong.

"So am I!" answered the clergyman sharply, while Strong threw himself into a chair, good-natured as ever, and said:

"Come along then! Will you go up with Wharton and me by the early train to-morrow?"

"Yes!" replied Hazard quickly. Then he paused; there were limits to his power and he began to feel them. "No!" he went on. "I can't get away to-morrow. I must wait till Sunday night."

"Better wait altogether," said Strong. "You take the chances against you."

"I told her I should follow her, and I shall," repeated Hazard stiffly. He felt hurt, as though Esther had rebelled against his authority, and he was not well pleased that Strong should volunteer advice.

"Give me my orders then!" said Strong. "Can I do any thing for you?"

"I shall be there on Monday afternoon. Telegraph me if they should decide to leave the place earlier. Try and keep them quiet till I get there!"

"Shall I tell them you are coming?"

"Not for your life!" answered Hazard impatiently. "Do all you can to soothe and quiet her. Hint that in my place you would come. Try to make her hope it, but not fear it."

"I will do all that to the letter," said Strong. "I feel partly responsible for getting you and Esther into this scrape, and am ready to go a long way to pull you through; but this done I stop. If Esther is in earnest, I must stand by her. Is that square?"

Hazard frowned severely and hesitated. "The real struggle is just coming," said he. "If you keep out of the way, I shall win. So far I have never failed with her. My influence over her to-day is greater than ever, or she would not try to run away from it. If you interfere I shall think it unkind and unfriendly."

To this Strong answered pleasantly enough, but as though his mind were quite made up: "I don't mean to interfere if I can help it, but I can't persecute Esther, if it is going to make her unhappy. As it is, I am likely to catch a scoring from my aunt for bringing you down on them, and undoing her work. I wish I were clear of the whole matter and Esther were a pillar of the church."

With this declaration of contingent neutrality, Strong went his way, and as he walked musingly back to his rooms, he muttered to himself that he had done quite as much for Hazard as the case would warrant: "What a trump the girl is, and what a good fight she is making! I believe I am getting to be in love with her myself, and if he gives it up--hum--yes, if he gives it up,--then of course Esther will go abroad and forget it."

Hazard's solitary thoughts were not quite so pointless. The danger of disappointment and defeat roused in him the instinct of martyrdom. He was sure that all mankind would suffer if he failed to get the particular wife he wanted. "It is not a selfish struggle," he thought. "It is a human soul I am trying to save, and I will do it in the teeth of all the powers of darkness. If I can but set right this systematically misguided conscience, the task is done. It is the affair of a moment when once the light comes;--A flash! A miracle! If I cannot wield this fire from Heaven, I am unfit to touch it. Let it burn me up!"

Early the next morning, not a little to their own surprise, Strong and Wharton found themselves dashing over the Erie Road towards Buffalo. They had a long day before them and luckily Wharton was in his best spirits. As for Strong he was always in good spirits. Within the memory of man, well or ill, on sea or shore, in peril or safety, Strong had never been seen unhappy or depressed. He had the faculty of interesting himself without an effort in the doings of his neighbors, and Wharton always had on hand some scheme which was to make an epoch in the history of art. Just now it was a question of a new academy of music which was to be the completest product of architecture, and to combine all the senses in delight. The Grand Opera at Paris was to be tame beside it. Here he was to be tied down by no such restraints as the church imposed on him; he was to have beauty for its own sake and to create the thought of a coming world. His decorations should make a revolution in the universe. Strong entered enthusiastically into his plans, but both agreed that preliminary studies were necessary both for architects and artists. The old world must be ransacked to the depths of Japan and Persia. Before their dinner-hour was reached, they had laid out a scheme of travel and study which would fill a life-time, while the Home of Music in New York was still untouched. After dinner and a cigar, they fought a prodigious battle over the influence of the Aryan races on the philosophy of art, and then, dusk coming on, they went to sleep, and finished an agreeable journey at about midnight.

When at last they drove up to the hotel door in the frosty night, and stamped their feet, chilled by the sleigh-ride from the station, the cataract's near roar and dim outline under the stars did not prevent them from warmly greeting Mr. Murray who sallied out to welcome them and to announce that their supper was waiting. The three women had long since gone to bed, but Mr. Murray staid up to have a chat with the boys. He was in high spirits. He owned that he had enjoyed his trip and was in no hurry to go home. While his nephew and Wharton attacked their supper, he sipped his Scotch whisky, and with the aid of a cigar, enlivened the feast.

"We got over here before three o'clock," said he, "and of course I took them out to drive at once. Esther sat in front with me and we let the horses go. Your aunt thinks I am unsafe with horses and I took some pains to prove that she was right. The girls liked it. They wouldn't have minded being tipped into a snow-bank, but I thought it would be rough on your aunt, so I brought them home safe, gave them a first-rate dinner and sent them off to bed hours ago, sleepy as gods. To-morrow you must take them in hand. I have made to-day what the newspapers call my most brilliant forensic effort, and I'll not risk my reputation again."

"Keep out of our way then!" said Strong. "Wharton and I mean to spill those two girls over the cliff unless Canadian horses know geology."

Esther slept soundly that night while the roar of the waters lulled her slumbers. The sun woke her the next morning to a sense of new life. Her room looked down on the cataract, and she had already taken a fancy to this tremendous, rushing, roaring companion, which thundered and smoked under her window, as though she had tamed a tornado to play in her court-yard. To brush her hair while such a confidant looked on and asked questions, was more than Pallas Athene herself could do, though she looked out forever from the windows of her Acropolis over the Blue AEgean. The sea is capricious, fickle, angry, fawning, violent, savage and wanton; it caresses and raves in a breath, and has its moods of silence, but Esther's huge playmate rambled on with its story, in the same steady voice, never shrill or angry, never silent or degraded by a sign of human failings, and yet so frank and sympathetic that she had no choice but to like it. "Even if it had nothing to tell me, its manners are divine," said Esther to herself as she leaned against the window sash and looked out. "And its dress!" she ran on. "What a complexion, to stand dazzling white and diamonds in the full sunlight!" Yet it was not the manners or the dress of her new friend that most won Esther's heart. Her excitement and the strain of the last month had left her subject to her nerves and imagination. She was startled by a snow-flake, was reckless and timid by turns, and her fancy ran riot in dreams of love and pain. She fell in love with the cataract and turned to it as a confidant, not because of its beauty or power, but because it seemed to tell her a story which she longed to understand. "I think I do understand it," she said to herself as she looked out. "If he could only hear it as I do," and of course "he" was Mr. Hazard; "how he would feel it!" She felt tears roll down her face as she listened to the voice of the waters and knew that they were telling her a different secret from any that Hazard could ever hear. "He will think it is the church talking!" Sad as she was, she smiled as she thought that it was Sunday morning, and a ludicrous contrast flashed on her mind between the decorations of St. John's, with its parterre of nineteenth century bonnets, and the huge church which was thundering its gospel under her eyes.

To have Niagara for a rival is no joke. Hazard spoke with no such authority; and Esther's next idea was one of wonder how, after listening here, any preacher could have the confidence to preach again. "What do they know about it?" she asked herself. "Which of them can tell a story like this, or a millionth part of it?" To dilute it in words and translate bits of it for school-girls, or to patronize it by defense or praise, was somewhat as though Esther herself should paint a row of her saints on the cliff under Table Rock. Even to fret about her own love affairs in such company was an impertinence. When eternity, infinity and omnipotence seem to be laughing and dancing in one's face, it is well to treat such visitors civilly, for they come rarely in such a humor.

So much did these thoughts interest and amuse her that she took infinite pains with her toilet in order to honor her colossal host whose own toilet was sparkling with all the jewels of nature, like an Indian prince whose robes are crusted with diamonds and pearls. When she came down to the breakfast-room, Strong, who was alone there, looked up with a start.

"Why, Esther!" he broke out, "take care, or one of these days you will be handsome!"

Catherine too was pretty as a fawn, and was so honestly pleased to meet Wharton again that he expanded into geniality. As for broken hearts, no self-respecting young woman shows such an ornament at any well regulated breakfast-table; they are kept in dark drawers and closets like other broken furniture. Esther had made the deadliest resolution to let no trace of her unhappiness appear before her uncle, and Mr. Murray, who saw no deeper than other men into the heart-problem, was delighted with the gayety of the table, and proud of his own success as a physician for heart complaints. Mrs. Murray, who knew more about her own sex, kept her eye on the two girls with more anxiety than she cared to confess. If any new disaster should happen, the prospect would be desperate, and it was useless to deny that she had taken risks heavy enough to stagger a professional gambler. The breakfast table looked gay and happy enough, and so did the rapids which sparkled and laughed in the distance.

After breakfast the two young women, with much preparation of boots, veils and wraps, went off with Strong and Wharton for a stroll down to the banks of the river. The two older members of the party remained quietly in their parlor, thinking that the young people would get on better by themselves. As the four wandered down the road, Mr. Murray watched them, and noticed the natural way in which Esther joined Strong, while Catherine fell to Wharton. Standing with his hands in his trousers' pockets and his nose close to the window-pane, Mr. Murray looked after them as they disappeared down the bank, and then, without turning round, he made a remark as husbands do, addressed to the universe and intended for his wife.

"I suppose that is what you are driving at."

"What?" asked Mrs. Murray.

"I don't mind George and Esther, but I grudge Catherine to that man Wharton. He may be a good artist, but I think his merits as a husband beneath criticism. I believe every woman would connive at a love affair though the man had half a dozen living wives, and had been hung two or three times for murder."

"I wish Esther were as safe as I think Catherine," said Mrs. Murray. "It would surprise me very much if Catherine took Mr. Wharton now, but if Mr. Hazard were to walk round the corner, I should expect to see Esther run straight into his arms."

"Hazard!" exclaimed Mr. Murray. "I thought he was out of the running and you meant Esther for George."

"I am not a match-maker, and I've no idea that Esther will ever marry George," replied Mrs. Murray with the patience which wives sometimes show to husbands whom they think obtuse.

"Then what is it you want?" asked Mr. Murray, with some signs of rebellion, but still talking to the window-pane, with his hands in his pockets. "You encourage a set of clever men to hang round two pretty girls, and you profess at the same time not to want anything to come of it. That kind of conduct strikes an ordinary mind as inconsistent."

"I want to prevent one unhappy marriage, not to make two," replied his wife. "Girls must have an education, and the only way they can get a good one is from clever men. As for falling in love, they will always do that whether the men are clever or not. They must take the risk."

"And what do you mean to do with them when they *are* educated?" inquired he.

"I mean them to marry dull, steady men in Wall Street, without any manners, and with their hands in their pockets," answered Mrs. Murray, her severity for once mingled with a touch of sweetness.

"Thank you," replied her husband, at last turning round. "Then that is to be the fruit of all this to-do?"

"I am sure it is quite fruit enough," rejoined she. "The business of educating their husbands will take all the rest of their lives."

Mr. Murray reflected a few minutes, standing with his back to the fire and gazing at his wife. Then he said: "Sarah, you are a clever woman. If you would come into my office and work steadily, you could double my income at the bar; but you need practice; your points are too fine; you run too many risks, and no male judge would ever support your management of a case. As practice I grant you it is bold and has much to recommend it, but in the law we cannot look so far ahead. Now, why won't you let Esther marry George?"

"I shall practice only before women judges," replied Mrs. Murray, "and I will undertake to say that I never should find one so stupid as not to see that George is not at all the sort of man whom a girl with Esther's notions would marry. If I tried to make her do it, I should be as wrong-headed as some men I know."

"I suppose you don't mean to put yourself in George's way, if he asks her," inquired Mr. Murray rather anxiously.

"My dear husband, there is no use in thinking about George one way or the other. Do put him out of your head! You fancy because Esther seems bright this morning, that she might marry George to-morrow. Now I can see a great deal more of Esther's mind than you, and I tell you that it is all we can do to prevent her from recalling Mr. Hazard, and that if we do prevent it, we shall have to take her abroad for at least two years before she gets over the strain."

At this emphatic announcement that his life was to be for two years a sacrifice to Esther's love-affairs, Mr. Murray retired again to his window and meditated in a more subdued spirit. He knew that protest would avail nothing.

Meanwhile the two girls were already down on the edge of the icy river, talking at first of the scene which lay before their eyes.

"Think what the Greeks would have done with it!" said Wharton. "They would have set Zeus in a throne on Table Rock, firing away his lightnings at Prometheus under the fall."

"Just for a change I rather like our way of sticking advertisements there," said Catherine. "It makes one feel at home."

"A woman feels most the kind of human life in it," said Esther.

"A big, rollicking, Newfoundland dog sort of humanity," said Strong.

"You are all wrong," said Catherine. "The fall is a woman, and she is as self-conscious this morning as if she were at church. Look at the coquetry of the pretty curve where the water falls over, and the lace on the skirt where it breaks into foam! Only a woman could do that and look so pretty when she might just as easily be hideous."

"It is not a woman! It is a man!" broke in Esther vehemently. "No woman ever had a voice like that!" She felt hurt that her cataract should be treated as a self-conscious woman.

"Now, Mr. Wharton!" cried Catherine, appealing to the artist: "Now, you see I'm right, and self-consciousness is sometimes a beauty."

Wharton answered this original observation of nature by a lecture which may be read to more advantage in his printed works. It ended by Catherine requiring him to draw for her the design of a dress which should have the soul of Niagara in its folds, and while he was engaged in this labor, which absorbed Catherine's thoughts and gave her extreme amusement, Esther strolled on with Strong, and for nearly an hour walked up and down the road, or leaned against the rock in sheltered places where the sun was warm. At first they went on talking of the scenery, then Esther wanted to know about the geology, and quickly broke in on Strong's remarks upon this subject by questions which led further and further away from it. The river boiled at their feet; the sun melted the enormous icicles which hung from the precipice behind them; a mass of frozen spray was banked up against the American fall opposite them, making it look like an iceberg, and snow covered every thing except the perpendicular river banks and the dark water. The rainbow hung over the cataract, and the mist rose from the furious waters into the peace of the quiet air.

"You know what has happened?" she asked.

Strong nodded assent. He was afraid to tell her how much he knew.

"Do you think I have done wrong?"

"How can I tell without knowing all your reasons?" he asked. "It looks to me as though you were uncertain of yourself and cared less for him than he for you. If I were in his place I should follow you close up, and refuse to leave you."

Esther gave a little gasp: "You don't think he will do that? if he does, I shall run away again."

"Why run away? if you really want to get rid of him, why not make him run away?"

"Because I don't want to make him run away from me, and because I don't know how. If I could only get him away from his church! All I know about it is that I can't be a clergyman's wife, but the moment that I try to explain why, he proves to me that my reasons are good for nothing."

"Are you sure he's not right?" asked Strong.

"Perfectly sure!" replied Esther earnestly. "I can't reason it out, but I feel it. I believe you could explain it if you would, but when I asked you, in the worst of my trouble, you refused to help me."

"I gave you all the help I could, and I am ready to give you whatever you want more," replied Strong.

"Tell me what you think about religion!"

Strong drew himself together with a perceptible effort: "I think about it as little as possible," said he.

"Do you believe in a God?"

"Not in a personal one."

"Or in future rewards and punishments?"

"Old women's nursery tales!"

"Do you believe in nothing?"

"There is evidence amounting to strong probability, of the existence of two things," said Strong, slowly, and as though in his lecture-room.

"What are they, if you please?"

"Should you know better if I said they were mind and matter?"

"You believe in nothing else?"

"N-N-No!" hesitated Strong.

"Isn't it horrible, your doctrine?"

"What of that, if it's true? I never said it was pleasant."

"Do you expect to convert any one to such a religion?"

"Great Buddha, no! I don't want to convert any one. I prefer almost any kind of religion. No one ever took up this doctrine who could help himself."

Esther pondered deeply for a time. Strong's trick of driving her to do what he wanted was so old a habit that she had learned to distrust it. At last she began again from another side.

"You really mean that this life is every thing, and the future nothing?"

"I never said so. I rather think the church is right in thinking this life nothing and the future every thing."

"But you deny a future life!"

Strong began to feel uncomfortable. He wanted to defend his opinions, and it became irksome to go on making out the strongest case he could against himself.

"Come!" said he: "don't go beyond what I said. I only denied the rewards and punishments. Mind! I'll not say there is a future life, but I don't deny it's possibility."

"You are willing to give us a chance?" said Esther rather sarcastically.

"I don't know that you would call it one," replied Strong satisfied by Esther's irony that he had now gone far enough. "If our minds could get hold of one abstract truth, they would be immortal so far as that truth is concerned. My trouble is to find out how we can get hold of the truth at all."

"My trouble is that I don't think I understand in the least what you mean," replied Esther.

"I thought you knew enough theology for that," said George. "The thing is simple enough. Hazard and I and every one else agree that thought is eternal. If you can get hold of one true thought, you are immortal as far as that thought goes. The only difficulty is that every fellow thinks his thought the true one. Hazard wants you to believe in his, and I don't want you to believe in mine, because I've not got one which I believe in myself."

"Still I don't understand," said Esther. "How can I make myself immortal by taking Mr. Hazard's opinions?"

"Because then the truth is a part of you! if I understand St. Paul, this is sound church doctrine, leaving out the personal part of the Trinity which Hazard insists on tacking to it. Except for the rubbish, I don't think I am so very far away from him," continued Strong, now assuming that he had done what he could to set Esther straight, and going on with the conversation as though it had no longer a personal interest. As he talked, he poked holes in the snow with his stick, as though what he said was for his own satisfaction, and he were turning this old problem over again in his mind to see whether he could find any thing new at the bottom of it. "I can't see that my ideas are so brutally shocking. We may some day catch an abstract truth by the tail, and then we shall have our religion and immortality. We have got far more than half way. Infinity is infinitely more intelligible to you than you are to a sponge. If the soul of a sponge can grow to be the soul of a Darwin, why may we not all grow up to abstract truth? What more do you want?"

As he looked up again, saying these words without thinking of Esther's interest, he was startled to see that this time she was listening with a very different expression in her face. She broke in with a question which staggered him.

"Does your idea mean that the next world is a sort of great reservoir of truth, and that what is true in us just pours into it like raindrops?"

"Well!" said he, alarmed and puzzled: "the figure is not perfectly correct, but the idea is a little of that kind."

"After all I wonder whether that may not be what Niagara has been telling me!" said Esther, and she spoke with an outburst of energy that made Strong's blood run cold.

Chapter X

S TRONG kept his word about amusing the two girls. They were not allowed the time to make themselves unhappy, restless or discontented. This Sunday afternoon he set out with a pair of the fastest horses to be got in the neighborhood, and if these did not go several times over the cliff, it was, as Strong had said, rather their own good sense than their driver's which held them back. Catherine, who sat by Strong's side, made the matter worse by taking the reins, and a more reckless little Amazon never defied men. Even Strong himself at one moment, when wreck seemed certain, asked her to kindly see to the publication of a posthumous memoir, and Esther declared that although she did not fear death, she disliked Catherine's way of killing her. Catherine paid no attention to such ribaldry, and drove on like Phaeton. Wharton was carried away by the girl's dash and coolness. He wanted to paint her as the charioteer of the cataract. They drove by the whirlpool, and so far and fast that, when Esther found herself that night tossing and feverish in her bed, she could only dream that she was still skurrying over a snowbound country, aching with jolts and jerks, but unable ever to stop. The next day she was glad to stay quietly in the house and amuse herself with sketching, while the rest of the party crossed the river to get Mr. Murray's sleeping-berth by the night train to New York, and to waste their time and money on the small attractions of the village. Mr. Murray was forced to return to his office. Wharton, who had no right to be here at all, for a score of pressing engagements were calling for instant attention in New York, telegraphed simply that his work would detain him several days longer at Niagara, and he even talked of returning with the others by way of Quebec.

While the rest of the party were attending to their own affairs at the railway station and the telegraph office, Wharton and Catherine strolled down to the little park over the American Fall and looked at the scene from there. Catherine in her furs was prettier than ever; her fresh color was brightened by the red handkerchief she had tied round her neck, and her eyes were more mutinous than usual. As she leaned over the parapet, and looked into the bubbling torrent which leaped into space at her feet, Wharton would have liked to carry her off like the torrent and give her no chance to resist. Yet, reckless as he was, he had still common sense enough to understand that, until he was fairly rid of one wife, he could not expect another to throw herself into his arms, and he awkwardly flitted about her, like a moth about a lantern, unable even to singe his wings in the flame.

"Then it is decided?" he asked. "You are really going abroad?"

"I am really going to take Esther to Europe for at least two years. We want excitement. America is too tame."

"May I come over and see you there?"

"No followers are to be allowed. I have forbidden Esther to think of them. She must devote all her time to art, or I shall be severe with her."

"But I suppose you don't mean to devote all your own time to art."

"I must take care of her," replied Catherine. "Then I have got to write some more sonnets. My hand is getting out in sonnets."

"Paris will spoil you; I shall wish you had never left your prairie," said Wharton sadly.

"It is you that have spoiled me," replied she. "You have made me self-conscious, and I am going abroad to escape your influence."

"Do me a favor when you are there; go to Avignon and Vaucluse; when you come to Petrarch's house, think of me, for there I passed the most hopeless hours of my life."

"No, I will not go there to be sad. Sadness is made only for poetry or painting. It is your affair, not mine. I mean to be gay."

"Try, then!" said Wharton. "See for yourself how far gayety will carry you. My turn will come! We all have to go over that cataract, and you will have to go over with the rest of us."

Catherine peered down into the spray and foam beneath as though she were watching herself fall, and then replied: "I shall stay in the shallowest puddle I can find."

"You will one day learn to give up your own life and follow an ideal," said Wharton.

Catherine laughed at his solemn speech with a boldness that irritated him. "Men are always making themselves into ideals and expecting women to follow them," said she. "You are all selfish. Tell me now honestly, would you not sell yourself and me and all New York, like Faust in the opera, if you could paint one picture like Titian?"

Wharton answered sulkily: "I would like to do it on Faust's conditions."

"I knew it," cried she exultingly.

"If ever the devil, or any one else," continued Wharton, "can get me to say to the passing moment, 'stay, thou art so fair,' he can have me for nothing. By that time I shall be worth nothing."

"Your temper will be much sweeter," interjected Catherine.

"Faust made a bargain that any man would be glad to make," growled Wharton. "It was not till he had no soul worth taking that the devil had a chance to win."

Catherine turned on him suddenly with her eyes full of humor: "Then that is the bargain you offer us women. You want us to take you on condition that we amuse you, and then you tell us that if we do amuse you, it will be because you are no longer worth taking. Thank you! I can amuse myself better. When we come home from Europe, I am going to buy a cattle ranche in Colorado and run it myself. You and Mr. Strong and Mr. Hazard shall come out there and see it. You will want me to take you on wages as cowboys. I mean to have ten thousand head, and when you see them you will say that they are better worth painting than all the saints and naiads round the Mediterranean."

Wharton looked earnestly at her for a moment before replying, and she met his eyes with a laugh that left him helpless. Unless taken seriously, he was beneath the level of average men. At last he closed the talk with a desperate confession of failure.

"If you will not go to Vaucluse, Miss Brooke, go at least to the British Museum in London, and when you are there, take a long look at what are called the Elgin marbles. There you will see Greek warriors killing each other with a smile on their faces. You remind me of them. You are like Achilles who answers his Trojan friend's prayer for life by saying: 'Die, friend; you are no better than others I have killed.' I mean to get Miss Dudley to give me her portrait of you, and I shall paint in, over your head: [Greek: PHILOS THANE KAI SY]; and hang it up in my studio to look at, when I am in danger of feeling happy."

With this they rambled back again towards their friends and ended for the time their struggle for mastery. The morning was soon over; all returned to their hotel, and luncheon followed; a silent meal at which no one seemed bright except Strong, who felt that the burden was beginning to be a heavy one. Had it not been for Strong, not one of the party would have moved out of the house again that day, but the Professor privately ordered a sleigh to the door at three o'clock, and packed his uncle and aunt into it together with Catherine and Wharton. Catherine's love of driving lent her energy, and Mrs. Murray, sadly enough, consented to let her take the reins. As they drove away, Strong stood on the porch and watched them till they had disappeared down the road. The afternoon was cloudy and gray, with flakes of snow dropping occasionally through a despondent air. After the sleigh had gone, Strong still gazed down the road, as though he expected to see something, but the road was bare.

He had stayed at home under the pretense of writing letters, and now returned to the sitting-room, where Esther was sketching from the window a view of the cataract. She went quietly on with her work, while he sat down to write as well as his conscience would allow him; for now that he saw how much good Esther's escape had done her, how quiet she had become again, and how her look of trouble had vanished, leaving only a tender little air of gravity, as she worked in the silence of her memories; and when he thought how violently this serenity was likely to be disturbed, his conscience smote him, he bitterly regretted his interference, and roundly denounced himself for a fool.

"Does Mr. Wharton really care for Catherine?" asked Esther, as she went on with her sketch.

"I guess he thinks he does," answered Strong. "He looks at her as though he would eat her."

"What a pity!"

"He is tough! Don't waste sympathy on him! If she took him, he would make her a slave within a week. As it is, his passion will go into his painting."

"She is a practical young savage," said Esther. "I thought at one time she was dazzled by him, but the moment she saw how unfit she was for such a man, she gave it up without a pang."

"I don't see her unfitness," replied Strong. "She has plenty of beauty, more common sense than he, and some money which would help him amazingly except that he would soon spend it. I should say it was he who wanted fitness, but you can't harness a mustang with a unicorn."

"He wants me to study in Paris," said Esther; "but I mean to go to Rome and Venice. I am afraid to tell him."

"When do you expect to be there?"

"Some time in May, if we can get any one to take us."

"Perhaps I will look you up in the summer. If I do not go to Oregon, I may run over to Germany."

"We shall be terribly homesick," replied Esther.

Silence now followed till Strong finished his letters and looked again at his watch. It was four o'clock. "If he is coming," thought Strong, "it is time he were here; but I would draw him a check for his church if he would stay away." The jingling of sleigh-bells made itself heard on the road below as though to rebuke him, and presently a cry of fright from Esther at the window told that she knew what was before her.

"What shall I do?" she cried breathlessly. "Here he is! I can't see him! I can't go through that scene again. George! won't you stop him?"

"What under the sun are you afraid of?" said Strong. "He'll not shoot you! If you don't mean to marry him, tell him so, and this time make it clear. Let there be no mistake about it! But don't send him away if you mean to make yourself unhappy afterwards."

"Of course I am going to be unhappy afterwards," groaned Esther. "What do you know about it, George? Do you think I feel about him as you would about a lump of coal? I was just beginning to be quiet and peaceful, and now it must all start up again. Go away! Leave us alone! But not long! If he is not gone within an hour, come back!"

The next instant the door opened and Hazard was shown into the room. His manner at this awkward moment was quiet and self-possessed, as though he had made it the business of his life to chase flying maidens. Having taken his own time, he was not to be thrown off his balance by any ordinary chance. He nodded familiarly to Strong, who left the room as he entered, and walking straight to Esther, held out his hand with a look of entreaty harder for her to resist than any form of reproach.

"I told you that I should follow," he said.

She drew back, raising her hand to check him, and putting on what she intended for a forbidding expression.

"It is my own fault. I should have spoken more plainly," she replied.

Instead of taking up the challenge, Hazard turned to the table where her unfinished drawing lay.

"What a good sketch!" he said, bending over it. "But you have not yet caught the real fall. I never saw an artist that had."

Esther's defense was disconcerted by this attack. Hazard was bent on getting back to his old familiar ground, and she let him take it. Her last hope was that he might be willing to take it, and be made content with it. If she could but persuade him to forget what had passed, and return to the footing of friendship which ought never to have been left! This was what she was made for! Her courage rose as she thought that perhaps this was possible, and as he sat down before the drawing and discussed it, she fancied that her object was already gained, and that this young greyhound at her elbow could be held in a leash and made to obey a sign.

In a few minutes he had taken again his old friendly place, and if she did not treat him with all the old familiarity, he still gained ground enough to warrant him in believing more firmly than ever that she could not resist his influence so long as he was at her side. They ran on together in talk about the drawing, until he felt that he might risk another approach, and his way of doing it was almost too easy and dexterous.

"What you want to get into your picture," he was saying; "is the air, which the fall has, of being something final. You can't go beyond Niagara. The universe seems made for it. Whenever I come here, I find myself repeating our sonnet: 'Siccome eterna vita e veder dio;' for the sight of it suggests eternity and infinite power." Then suddenly putting down the drawing, and looking up to her face, as she stood by his side, he said: "Do you know, I feel now for the first time the beauty of the next two verses:

'So, lady, sight of you, in my despair,   Brings paradise to this brief life and frail.'"

"Hush!" said Esther, raising her hand again; "we are friends now and nothing more."

"Mere friends, are we?" quoted Hazard, with a courageous smile. "No!" he went on quickly. "I love you. I cannot help loving you. There is no friendship about it."

"If you tell me so, I must run away again. I shall leave the room. Remember! I am terribly serious now."

"If you tell me, honestly and seriously, that you love me no longer and want me to go away, I will leave the room myself," answered Hazard.

"I won't say that unless you force me to it, but I expect you from this time to help me in carrying out what you know is my duty."

"I will promise, on condition that you prove to me first what your duty is."

To come back again to their starting point was not encouraging, and they felt it, but this time Esther was determined to be obeyed even if it cost her a lover as well as a husband. She did not flinch.

"What more proof do you need? I am not fit to be a clergyman's wife. I should be a scandal in the church, and you would have to choose between it and me."

"I know you better," said Hazard calmly. "You will find all your fears vanish if you once boldly face them."

"I have tried," said Esther. "I tried desperately and failed utterly."

"Try once more! Do not turn from all that has been the hope and comfort of men, until you have fairly learned what it is!"

"Is it not enough to know myself?" asked Esther. "Some people are made with faith. I am made without it."

Hazard broke in here in a warmer tone: "I know you better than you know yourself! Do you think that I, whose business it is to witness every day of my life the power of my faith, am going to hesitate before a trifle like your common, daily, matter-of-course fears and doubts, such as have risen and been laid in every mind that was worth being called one, ever since minds existed?"

"Have they always been laid?" asked Esther gravely.

"Always!" answered Hazard firmly; "provided the doubter wanted to lay them. It is a simple matter of will!"

"Would you have gone into the ministry if you had been tormented by them as I am?" she asked.

"I am not afraid to lay bare my conscience to you," he replied becoming cool again, and willing perhaps to stretch his own points of conscience in the effort to control hers. "I suppose the clergyman hardly exists who has not been tormented by doubts. As for myself, if I could have removed my doubts by so simple a step as that of becoming an atheist, I should have done it, no matter what scandal or punishment had followed. I studied the subject thoroughly, and found that for one doubt removed, another was raised, only to reach at last a result more inconceivable than that reached by the church, and infinitely more hopeless besides. What do you gain by getting rid of one incomprehensible only to put a greater one in its place, and throw away your only hope besides? The atheists offer no sort of bargain for one's soul. Their scheme is all loss and no gain. At last both they and I come back to a confession of ignorance; the only difference between us is that my ignorance is joined with a faith and hope."

Esther was staggered by this view of the subject, and had to fall back on her common-places: "But you make me say every Sunday that I believe in things I don't believe at all."

"But I suppose you believe at last in something, do you not?" asked Hazard. "Somewhere there must be common ground for us to stand on; and our church makes very large--I think too large, allowances for difference. For my own part, I accept tradition outright, because I think it wiser to receive a mystery than to weaken faith; but no one exacts such strictness from you. There are scores of cler-gymen to-day in our pulpits who are in my eyes little better than open skeptics, yet I am not allowed to refuse communion with them. Why should you refuse it with me? You must at last trust in some mysterious and humanly incomprehensible form of words. Even Strong has to do this. Why may you not take mine?"

"I hardly know what to trust in," said Esther sadly.

"Then trust in me."

"I wish I could, but--"

"But what? Tell me frankly where your want of confidence lies."

"I want to tell you, but I'm afraid. This is what has stood between us from the first. If I told you what was on my lips, you would think it an insult. Don't drive me into offending you! If you knew how much I want to keep your friendship, you would not force me to say such things."

"I will not be offended," answered Hazard gayly. "I can stand almost any thing except being told that you no longer love me."

It wrung Esther's heart to throw away a love so pure and devoted. She felt ashamed of her fears and of herself. As he spoke, her ears seemed to hear a running echo: "Mistress, know yourself! Down on your knees, and thank heaven fasting for a good man's love!" She sat some moments silent while he gazed into her face, and her eyes wandered out to the gloomy and cloud-covered cataract. She felt herself being swept over it. Whichever way she moved, she had to look down into an abyss, and leap.

"Spare me!" she said at last. "Why should you drive and force me to take this leap? Are all men so tyrannical with women? You do not quarrel with a man because he cannot give you his whole life."

"I own it!" said Hazard warmly. "I am tyrannical! I want your whole life, and even more. I will be put off with nothing else. Don't you see that I can't retreat? Put yourself in my place! Think how you would act if you loved me as I love you!"

"Ah, be generous!" begged Esther. "It is not my fault if you and your profession are one; and of all things on earth, to be half-married must be the worst torture."

"You are perfectly right," he replied. "My profession and I are one, and this makes my case harder, for I have to fight two battles, one of love, and one of duty. Think for a moment what a struggle it is! I love you passionately. I would like to say to you: 'Take me on your own terms! I will give you my life, as I will take yours.' But how can I? You are trembling on the verge of what I think destruction. If I saw you tossing on the rapids yonder, at the edge of the fall, I could not be more eager to save you. Yet think what self-control I have had to exercise, for though I have felt myself, for weeks, fighting a battle of life and death for a soul much dearer to me than my own, I have gone forward as though I felt no alarm. I have never even spoken to you on the subject. I stood by, believing so entirely in you that I dared let your own nature redeem itself. But now you throw out a challenge, and I have no choice but to meet it. I have got to fight for myself and my profession and you, at the same time."

At last, then, the battle was fairly joined, and desperately as both the lovers had struggled against it, they looked their destiny in the face. With all Esther's love and sympathy for Hazard, and with all the subtle power which his presence had on her will, his last speech was unlucky. Here was what she had feared! She seemed to feel now, what she had only vaguely suspected before, the restraint which would be put upon her the moment she should submit to his will. He had as good as avowed that nothing but the fear of losing her had kept him silent. She fancied that the thunders of the church were already rolling over her head, and that her mind was already slowly shutting itself up under the checks of its new surroundings. Hazard's speech, too, was unlucky in another way. If he had tried not to shock her by taking charge of her soul before she asked for his interference, she had herself made a superhuman effort not to shock him, and never once had she let drop a word that could offend his prejudices. Since the truth must now come out, she was the less anxious to spare his pride because he claimed credit for respecting hers.

"Must you know why I have broken down and run away?" she said at last. "Well! I will tell you. It was because, after a violent struggle with myself, I found I could not enter a church without a feeling of--of hostility. I can only be friendly by staying away from it. I felt as though it were part of a different world. You will be angry with me for saying it, but I never saw you conduct a service without feeling as though you were a priest in a Pagan temple, centuries apart from me. At any moment I half expected to see you bring out a goat or a ram and sacrifice it on the high altar. How could I, with such ideas, join you at communion?"

No wonder that Esther should have hesitated! Her little speech was not meant in ridicule of Hazard, but it stung him to the quick. He started up and walked across the room to the window, where he stood a moment trying to recover his composure.

"What you call Pagan is to me proof of an eternal truth handed down by tradition and divine revelation," he said at length. "But the mere ceremonies need not stand in your way. Surely you can disregard them and feel the truths behind."

"Oh, yes!" answered Esther, plunging still deeper into the morass. "The ceremonies are picturesque and I could get used to them, but the doctrines are more Pagan than the ceremonies. Now I have hurt your feelings enough, and will say no more. What I have said proves that I am not fit to be your wife. Let me go in peace!"

Again Hazard thought a moment with a grave face. Then he said: "Every church

is open to the same kind of attack you make on ours. Do you mean to separate yourself from all communion?"

"If you will create a new one that shall be really spiritual, and not cry: 'flesh--
flesh--flesh,' at every corner, I will gladly join it, and give my whole life to you and
it."

Hazard shook his head: "I can suggest nothing more spiritual than what came
from the spirit itself, and has from all time satisfied the purest and most spiritual
souls."

"If I could make myself contented with what satisfied them, I would do it for
your sake," answered Esther. "It must be that we are in a new world now, for I can
see nothing spiritual about the church. It is all personal and selfish. What difference
does it make to me whether I worship one person, or three persons, or three hundred, or three thousand. I can't understand how you worship any person at all."

Hazard literally groaned, and his involuntary expression so irritated Esther that
she ran on still more recklessly.

"Do you really believe in the resurrection of the body?" she asked.

"Of course I do!" replied Hazard stiffly.

"To me it seems a shocking idea. I despise and loathe myself, and yet you thrust
self at me from every corner of the church as though I loved and admired it. All
religion does nothing but pursue me with self even into the next world."

Esther had become very animated in the course of her remarks, and not the
less so because she saw Hazard frown and make gestures of impatience as she passed
from one sacrilege to another. At last he turned at bay, and broke out:

"Do you think all this is new to me? I know by heart all these criticisms of the
church. I have heard them in one form and another ever since I was a boy at school.
They are all equally poor and ignorant. They touch no vital point, for they are made
by men, like your cousin George Strong, from whom I suppose you got them, who
know nothing of the church or its doctrines or its history. I'll not argue over them.
Let them go for whatever you may think they are worth. I will only put to you one
question and no more. If you answer it against me, I will go away, and never annoy
you again. You say the idea of the resurrection is shocking to you. Can you, without
feeling still more shocked, think of a future existence where you will not meet once
more father or mother, husband or children? surely the natural instincts of your sex

must save you from such a creed!"

"Ah!" cried Esther, almost fiercely, and blushing crimson, as though Hazard this time had pierced the last restraint on her self-control: "Why must the church always appeal to my weakness and never to my strength! I ask for spiritual life and you send me back to my flesh and blood as though I were a tigress you were sending back to her cubs. What is the use of appealing to my sex? the atheists at least show me respect enough not to do that!"

At this moment the door opened and Strong entered. It was high time. The scene threatened to become almost violent. As Strong came in, Esther was standing by the fire-place, all her restless features flashing with the excitement of her last speech. Hazard, with his back to the window, was looking at her across the room, his face dark with displeasure. As Strong stepped between them, a momentary silence followed, when not a sound was heard except the low thunder of the falling waters. One would have said that storm was in the air. Suddenly Hazard turned on the unlucky professor and hurled at him the lightning.

"You are the cause of all this! what is your motive?"

Strong looked at him with surprise, but understood in a moment what had happened. Seeing himself destined in any case to be the victim of the coming wrath, he quietly made up his mind to bear the lot of all mediators and inter-meddlers.

"I am afraid you are half right," he answered. "My stupidity may have made matters a little worse."

"What was your motive?" repeated Hazard sternly.

"My motive was to fight your battle for you," replied Strong unruffled; "and I did it clumsily, that's all! I might have known it beforehand."

"Have you been trying to supplant me in order to get yourself in my place?" demanded Hazard, still in the tone of a master.

"No!" replied Strong, half inclined to laugh.

"You will never find happiness there!" continued Hazard, turning to Esther, and pointing with a sweep of his hand to Strong.

"Esther agrees with you on that point," said Strong, beginning to think it time that this scene should end. "I don't mind telling you, too, that since I have seen her stand out against your persecution, I would give any chance I have of salvation if she would marry me; but you needn't be alarmed about it,--she won't!"

"She will!" broke in Hazard abruptly. "You have betrayed me, and your conduct is all of a piece with your theories." Then turning to Esther, who still stood motionless and silent before the fire, he went on: "I am beaten. You have driven me away, and I will never trouble you again, till, in your days of suffering and anguish you send to me for hope and consolation. Till then--God bless you!"

The silence was awful when his retreating footsteps could no longer be heard. It was peace, but the peace of despair. As the sound of the jangling sleigh-bells slowly receded from the door, and Esther realized that the romance of her life was ended, she clasped her hands together in a struggle to control her tears. Strong walked once or twice up and down the room, buried in thought, then suddenly stopping before her, he said in his straight-forward, practical way:

"Esther, I meant it! you have fought your battle like a heroine. If you will marry me, I will admire and love you more than ever a woman was loved since the world began."

Esther looked at him with an expression that would have been a smile if it had not been infinitely dreary and absent; then she said, simply and finally:

"But George, I don't love you, I love him."

THE END.

www.bookjungle.com *email: sales@bookjungle.com fax: 630-214-0564 mail: Book Jungle PO Box 2226 Champaign, IL 61825*

The Codes Of Hammurabi And Moses
W. W. Davies

QTY

The discovery of the Hammurabi Code is one of the greatest achievements of archaeology, and is of paramount interest, not only to the student of the Bible, but also to all those interested in ancient history...

Religion **ISBN:** *1-59462-338-4* **Pages:**132
MSRP $12.95

The Theory of Moral Sentiments
Adam Smith

QTY

This work from 1749. contains original theories of conscience amd moral judgment and it is the foundation for systemof morals.

Philosophy **ISBN:** *1-59462-777-0* **Pages:**536
MSRP $19.95

Jessica's First Prayer
Hesba Stretton

QTY

In a screened and secluded corner of one of the many railway-bridges which span the streets of London there could be seen a few years ago, from five o'clock every morning until half past eight, a tidily set-out coffee-stall, consisting of a trestle and board, upon which stood two large tin cans, with a small fire of charcoal burning under each so as to keep the coffee boiling during the early hours of the morning when the work-people were thronging into the city on their way to their daily toil...

Childrens **ISBN:** *1-59462-373-2* **Pages:**84
MSRP $9.95

My Life and Work
Henry Ford

QTY

Henry Ford revolutionized the world with his implementation of mass production for the Model T automobile. Gain valuable business insight into his life and work with his own auto-biography... "We have only started on our development of our country we have not as yet, with all our talk of wonderful progress, done more than scratch the surface. The progress has been wonderful enough but..."

Biographies/ **ISBN:** *1-59462-198-5* **Pages:**300
MSRP $21.95

www.bookjungle.com *email: sales@bookjungle.com fax: 630-214-0564 mail: Book Jungle PO Box 2226 Champaign, IL 61825*

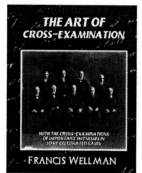

The Art of Cross-Examination
Francis Wellman

QTY

I presume it is the experience of every author, after his first book is published upon an important subject, to be almost overwhelmed with a wealth of ideas and illustrations which could readily have been included in his book, and which to his own mind, at least, seem to make a second edition inevitable. Such certainly was the case with me; and when the first edition had reached its sixth impression in five months, I rejoiced to learn that it seemed to my publishers that the book had met with a sufficiently favorable reception to justify a second and considerably enlarged edition. ..

Pages:412

Reference   ISBN: *1-59462-647-2*   *MSRP $19.95*

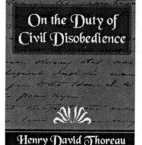

On the Duty of Civil Disobedience
Henry David Thoreau

QTY

Thoreau wrote his famous essay, On the Duty of Civil Disobedience, as a protest against an unjust but popular war and the immoral but popular institution of slave-owning. He did more than write—he declined to pay his taxes, and was hauled off to gaol in consequence. Who can say how much this refusal of his hastened the end of the war and of slavery ?

Law   ISBN: *1-59462-747-9*   **Pages:48**

MSRP $7.45

Dream Psychology Psychoanalysis for Beginners
Sigmund Freud

QTY

Sigmund Freud, born Sigismund Schlomo Freud (May 6, 1856 - September 23, 1939), was a Jewish-Austrian neurologist and psychiatrist who co-founded the psychoanalytic school of psychology. Freud is best known for his theories of the unconscious mind, especially involving the mechanism of repression; his redefinition of sexual desire as mobile and directed towards a wide variety of objects; and his therapeutic techniques, especially his understanding of transference in the therapeutic relationship and the presumed value of dreams as sources of insight into unconscious desires.

Pages:196

Psychology   ISBN: *1-59462-905-6*   *MSRP $15.45*

The Miracle of Right Thought
Orison Swett Marden

QTY

Believe with all of your heart that you will do what you were made to do. When the mind has once formed the habit of holding cheerful, happy, prosperous pictures, it will not be easy to form the opposite habit. It does not matter how improbable or how far away this realization may see, or how dark the prospects may be, if we visualize them as best we can, as vividly as possible, hold tenaciously to them and vigorously struggle to attain them, they will gradually become actualized, realized in the life. But a desire, a longing without endeavor, a yearning abandoned or held indifferently will vanish without realization.

Pages:360

Self Help   ISBN: *1-59462-644-8*   *MSRP $25.45*

QTY

The Rosicrucian Cosmo-Conception Mystic Christianity *by Max Heindel*   ISBN: *1-59462-188-8* **$38.95**
The Rosicrucian Cosmo-conception is not dogmatic, neither does it appeal to any other authority than the reason of the student. It is: not controversial, but is: sent forth in the, hope that it may help to clear...   *New Age/Religion Pages 646*

Abandonment To Divine Providence *by Jean-Pierre de Caussade*   ISBN: *1-59462-228-0* **$25.95**
"The Rev. Jean Pierre de Caussade was one of the most remarkable spiritual writers of the Society of Jesus in France in the 18th Century. His death took place at Toulouse in 1751. His works have gone through many editions and have been republished...   *Inspirational/Religion Pages 400*

Mental Chemistry *by Charles Haanel*   ISBN: *1-59462-192-6* **$23.95**
Mental Chemistry allows the change of material conditions by combining and appropriately utilizing the power of the mind. Much like applied chemistry creates something new and unique out of careful combinations of chemicals the mastery of mental chemistry...   *New Age Pages 354*

The Letters of Robert Browning and Elizabeth Barret Barrett 1845-1846 vol II   ISBN: *1-59462-193-4* **$35.95**
by Robert Browning and Elizabeth Barrett   *Biographies Pages 596*

Gleanings In Genesis (volume I) *by Arthur W. Pink*   ISBN: *1-59462-130-6* **$27.45**
Appropriately has Genesis been termed "the seed plot of the Bible" for in it we have, in germ form, almost all of the great doctrines which are afterwards fully developed in the books of Scripture which follow...   *Religion/Inspirational Pages 420*

The Master Key *by L. W. de Laurence*   ISBN: *1-59462-001-6* **$30.95**
In no branch of human knowledge has there been a more lively increase of the spirit of research during the past few years than in the study of Psychology. Concentration and Mental Discipline. The requests for authentic lessons in Thought Control, Mental Discipline and...   *New Age/Business Pages 422*

The Lesser Key Of Solomon Goetia *by L. W. de Laurence*   ISBN: *1-59462-092-X* **$9.95**
This translation of the first book of the "Lernegton" which is now for the first time made accessible to students of Talismanic Magic was done, after careful collation and edition, from numerous Ancient Manuscripts in Hebrew, Latin, and French...   *New Age/Occult Pages 92*

Rubaiyat Of Omar Khayyam *by Edward Fitzgerald*   ISBN:*1-59462-332-5* **$13.95**
Edward Fitzgerald, whom the world has already learned, in spite of his own efforts to remain within the shadow of anonymity, to look upon as one of the rarest poets of the century, was born at Bredfield, in Suffolk, on the 31st of March, 1809. He was the third son of John Purcell...   *Music Pages 172*

Ancient Law *by Henry Maine*   ISBN: *1-59462-128-4* **$29.95**
The chief object of the following pages is to indicate some of the earliest ideas of mankind, as they are reflected in Ancient Law, and to point out the relation of those ideas to modern thought.   *Religion/History Pages 452*

Far-Away Stories *by William J. Locke*   ISBN: *1-59462-129-2* **$19.45**
"Good wine needs no bush, but a collection of mixed vintages does. And this book is just such a collection. Some of the stories I do not want to remain buried for ever in the museum files of dead magazine-numbers an author's not unpardonable vanity..."   *Fiction Pages 272*

Life of David Crockett *by David Crockett*   ISBN: *1-59462-250-7* **$27.45**
"Colonel David Crockett was one of the most remarkable men of the times in which he lived. Born in humble life, but gifted with a strong will, an indomitable courage, and unremitting perseverance...   *Biographies/New Age Pages 424*

Lip-Reading *by Edward Nitchie*   ISBN: *1-59462-206-X* **$25.95**
Edward B. Nitchie, founder of the New York School for the Hard of Hearing, now the Nitchie School of Lip-Reading, Inc, wrote "LIP-READING Principles and Practice". The development and perfecting of this meritorious work on lip-reading was an undertaking...   *How-to Pages 400*

A Handbook of Suggestive Therapeutics, Applied Hypnotism, Psychic Science   ISBN: *1-59462-214-0* **$24.95**
by Henry Munro   *Health/New Age/Health/Self-help Pages 376*

A Doll's House: and Two Other Plays *by Henrik Ibsen*   ISBN: *1-59462-112-8* **$19.95**
Henrik Ibsen created this classic when in revolutionary 1848 Rome. Introducing some striking concepts in playwriting for the realist genre, this play has been studied the world over.   *Fiction/Classics/Plays 308*

The Light of Asia *by sir Edwin Arnold*   ISBN: *1-59462-204-3* **$13.95**
In this poetic masterpiece, Edwin Arnold describes the life and teachings of Buddha. The man who was to become known as Buddha to the world was born as Prince Gautama of India but he rejected the worldly riches and abandoned the reigns of power when...   *Religion/History/Biographies Pages 170*

The Complete Works of Guy de Maupassant *by Guy de Maupassant*   ISBN: *1-59462-157-8* **$16.95**
"For days and days, nights and nights, I had dreamed of that first kiss which was to consecrate our engagement, and I knew not on what spot I should put my lips..."   *Fiction/Classics Pages 240*

The Art of Cross-Examination *by Francis L. Wellman*   ISBN: *1-59462-309-0* **$26.95**
Written by a renowned trial lawyer, Wellman imparts his experience and uses case studies to explain how to use psychology to extract desired information through questioning.   *How-to/Science/Reference Pages 408*

Answered or Unanswered? *by Louisa Vaughan*   ISBN: *1-59462-248-5* **$10.95**
Miracles of Faith in China   *Religion Pages 112*

The Edinburgh Lectures on Mental Science (1909) *by Thomas*   ISBN: *1-59462-008-3* **$11.95**
This book contains the substance of a course of lectures recently given by the writer in the Queen Street Hall, Edinburgh. Its purpose is to indicate the Natural Principles governing the relation between Mental Action and Material Conditions...   *New Age/Psychology Pages 148*

Ayesha *by H. Rider Haggard*   ISBN: *1-59462-301-5* **$24.95**
Verily and indeed it is the unexpected that happens! Probably if there was one person upon the earth from whom the Editor of this, and of a certain previous history, did not expect to hear again...   *Classics Pages 380*

Ayala's Angel *by Anthony Trollope*   ISBN: *1-59462-352-X* **$29.95**
The two girls were both pretty; but Lucy who was twenty-one who supposed to be simple and comparatively unattractive, whereas Ayala was credited, as her Bombwhat romantic name might show, with poetic charm and a taste for romance. Ayala when her father died was nineteen...   *Fiction Pages 484*

The American Commonwealth *by James Bryce*   ISBN: *1-59462-286-8* **$34.45**
An interpretation of American democratic political theory. It examines political mechanics and society from the perspective of Scotsman James Bryce   *Politics Pages 572*

Stories of the Pilgrims *by Margaret P. Pumphrey*   ISBN: *1-59462-116-0* **$17.95**
This book explores pilgrims religious oppression in England as well as their escape to Holland and eventual crossing to America on the Mayflower, and their early days in New England...   *History Pages 268*

QTY

The Fasting Cure *by Sinclair Upton*
In the Cosmopolitan Magazine for May, 1910, and in the Contemporary Review (London) for April, 1910, I published an article dealing with my experiences in fasting. I have written a great many magazine articles, but never one which attracted so much attention... New Age/Self Help/Health Pages 164

ISBN: *1-59462-222-1* **$13.95** ☐

Hebrew Astrology *by Sepharial*
In these days of advanced thinking it is a matter of common observation that we have left many of the old landmarks behind and that we are now pressing forward to greater heights and to a wider horizon than that which represented the mind-content of our progenitors... Astrology Pages 144

ISBN: *1-59462-308-2* **$13.45** ☐

Thought Vibration or The Law of Attraction in the Thought World
by William Walker Atkinson

Psychology/Religion Pages 144

ISBN: *1-59462-127-6* **$12.95** ☐

Optimism *by Helen Keller*
Helen Keller was blind, deaf, and mute since 19 months old, yet famously learned how to overcome these handicaps, communicate with the world, and spread her lectures promoting optimism. An inspiring read for everyone... Biographies/Inspirational Pages 84

ISBN: *1-59462-108-X* **$15.95** ☐

Sara Crewe *by Frances Burnett*
In the first place, Miss Minchin lived in London. Her home was a large, dull, tall one, in a large, dull square, where all the houses were alike, and all the sparrows were alike, and where all the door-knockers made the same heavy sound... Childrens/Classic Pages 88

ISBN: *1-59462-360-0* **$9.45** ☐

The Autobiography of Benjamin Franklin *by Benjamin Franklin*
The Autobiography of Benjamin Franklin has probably been more extensively read than any other American historical work, and no other book of its kind has had such ups and downs of fortune. Franklin lived for many years in England, where he was agent... Biographies/History Pages 332

ISBN: *1-59462-135-7* **$24.95** ☐

Name	
Email	
Telephone	
Address	
City, State ZIP	

☐ **Credit Card**   ☐ **Check / Money Order**

Credit Card Number	
Expiration Date	
Signature	

Please Mail to: Book Jungle
PO Box 2226
Champaign, IL 61825
or Fax to: 630-214-0564

ORDERING INFORMATION
web*: www.bookjungle.com*
email*: sales@bookjungle.com*
fax*: 630-214-0564*
mail*: Book Jungle PO Box 2226 Champaign, IL 61825*
or PayPal *to sales@bookjungle.com*

Please contact us for bulk discounts

DIRECT-ORDER TERMS

**20% Discount if You Order
Two or More Books**
Free Domestic Shipping!
Accepted: Master Card, Visa,
Discover, American Express

Printed in the United States
98995LV00004B/41-80/A